China Jeep Patrol

~

Guadalcanal Diary

By Don Gardner

China Jeep Patrol

Guadalcanal Diary

By Don Gardner

Compiled together by Clinton Gardner

ISBN: 978-1-71684-085-2

Lulu.com

Lulu Press

627 Davis Dr STE 300

Morrisville, NC 27560-7101

http://www.lulu.com

Additional Lulu Contact Information:
Fax Numbers:(919) 459-5867; (919) 447-3198
Phone Numbers(919) 836-1950; (919) 447-3244

Manufactured in the United States of America

4

Table of Contents

Acknowledgements

I'd like to thank Jim Gardner for his assistance in the completion of this project. His help in providing materials, editing, research, military terminology and expertise; and most importantly answering the numerous questions and requests from me during the creation of this book.

I'd also like to thank Lynn Gardner Sims, Bethany Gardner-Rose, and Graciela Gardner-Beringer for their assistance in completing portions of this book.

In loving memory of Carole Kay Gardner,

the oldest daughter of Don Gardner.

We can't wait to see her again.

Another Gardner Family Book

Available at: www.Lulu.com

https://www.lulu.com/en/us/shop/art-gardner/the-characters-of-browns-park/hardcover/product-1kwvrmw7.html

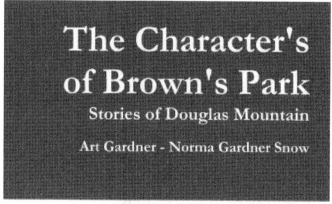

The Character's of Brown's Park

Stories of Douglas Mountain

Art Gardner - Norma Gardner Snow

Foreword

Arthur Donald Gardner wrote "Guadalcanal Diary," published in "The Rand McNally Almanac of Adventure" and "Soldier of Fortune" magazine.

Days after the infamous Japanese attack on Pearl Harbor, Gardner stood in a blocks-long line to join the Marine Corps. During his basic training, he volunteered for Carlson's Raiders. He participated in amphibious landings on Guadalcanal and Bougainville. He was medically evacuated off Bougainville due to malaria. While recovering in a San Diego Hospital, he was assigned to a Marine Military Police unit. He then served on Okinawa until the war ended. He was then sent to Tangku, China where he engaged in a Jeep Patrol. "China Jeep Patrol" is based on Gardner's experiences in the Tangku area in 1945.

Gardner entered the Marine Corps with an 8th grade education. After his discharge from the Marines, he earned an Associate Degree at Boise Junior College. He progressed to Denver University and finally Colorado State University.

Gardner's participation as a combat Marine and a Military Police Officer in Tangku, China provided him a unique perspective of the dangerous and desperate conditions in post WWII China.

~Foreword by James A. Gardner

CHINA

JEEP

PATROL

By Don Gardner

We always started the jeep patrol at 1900 hours, Casey and I, and cruised until 2300 hours. Every third day we switched with the other patrols to break the monotony. The night patrol was intended to enforce the 2200 curfew as much as possible. If the Marines were on the streets or in the whore houses, we nabbed them and hauled them in. If they were shacked up somewhere besides the houses, that was something else, and there was nothing we could do about it.

* * * * * *

The weather was still nice with only a hint that winter was coming. It was September 1945. The electric light system here in Tangku, China, left a lot to be desired and the jeep patrol could be spooky at times. Tangku was a small town at the mouth of the Yongdinghe River on the Yellow Sea. Thirty miles up the river was Tientsin and some one hundred miles further inland was Peiping. Everything was hooked together by railroad track and distance. The trains chugged faithfully back and forth carrying Chinese people from one place to another, most of them trying to avoid the war that was escalating between the Nationalists and the Reds.

Casey and I were Marine buck sergeants and this is what Marines have been calling "good duty" for a long time. Outside of our days to pull patrol, we did not do much of anything. We were billeted in "the compound" as we called it. It had been built by French troops sometime in the past and was surrounded by a red stone fence about twelve feet high with one main gate leading outside. Inside were some thirty buildings for the troops, all with verandas and dirt floors. It would accommodate no more than two hundred men and officers at the most and we were comfortable with just under one hundred forty. We were on detached duty and the rest of the battalion was stationed in Tientsin.

Our commanding officer was a captain who underneath the uniform and bars was a civilian at heart. He was enjoying China duty with every fiber of his being. His name was Pollard and things had to get pretty bad before he would so much as issue a reprimand. We appreciated him in a way and tried to make his command as problem free as we possibly could. It helped everyone.

We altered our patrol route from time to time to keep erring Marines and Sailors on their toes. I always drove, not that it made any difference, but we had started out that way and it worked well for both of us. Casey could catapult out of that front seat with almost no effort when necessary and be there looking trouble in the eye while I was stopping the jeep and unwinding from under the wheel.

This night I heard Casey say, "Something!" When he said, "Something" in that tone you could bet that it would be something alright. I glanced at him and he pointed ahead on the right. Then I spotted it. Someone was running away from us up the street and disappearing into the dark. Just ahead of us something or someone was lying in the street. I stopped alongside and Casey crawled out with the flashlight. It was a Marine and he was very dead. A bullet had hit him high in the back and came out through the softness of his throat. It left a hole as large as a half dollar. Casey had the flashlight beamed on his face and we watched his color drain away and the lines from his nose to his mouth deepen. He was bleeding from the wound in his back and the blood was beginning to seep out from under him.

I told Casey, "I'll stay here and you go get the Officer of the Day."

"Will you be alright?"

"I'll be fine."

"Are you sure?" asked Casey. We liked each other.

"Positive."

Casey got in the jeep, turned around and drove away into the dark.

* * * * * *

I put my back to the wall of a building there and waited. I had been overseas more than thirty-one months in two cruises. I was a combat Marine and combat was where they put me. I had gone through five major engagements and when the war was over, I was on Guam wondering where we would hit next. I was wounded twice; the first time on Guadalcanal when a piece of shrapnel took a chunk out of my left thigh. I raised hell when they tried to ship me to a hospital in Suva, Fiji Islands. I didn't want to leave my outfit and our Navy doctors finally decided to take care of it. The wound would have been prettier with plastic surgery to fill the hole, but it healed well and didn't bother me too much.

The second time came on Bougainville when a Japanese bullet hit my steel helmet on a level with my forehead. If anyone tries to tell you a bullet

12

won't penetrate a steel helmet, you can tell them for me that they are wrong. The bullet hit the front of my helmet at an angle, took off a piece of my scalp and exited out the back. It sounded like it must sound to have a bucket over your head, and someone hit it with a steel bat. My ears were ringing for a week.

I thought they might send me back to the States now that the war was over, but I was a regular rather than a reserve and still had five months of my enlistment to do, so they sent me to China to help ship the Japanese soldiers there back to Japan.

* * * * * *

I could see Casey coming back up the street and another jeep behind him. It was Capt. Pollard and he had a corporal and a PFC riding with him. Capt. Pollard hemmed and hawed and clicked his teeth and finally told two Marines to load the dead Marine in the back of his jeep and they drove away. We never did find out who had fired the shot. They were pretty sure the weapon was a .45 regulation pistol, the same as we carried on patrol, because of the size of the hole, but they never knew for sure. It could have been anyone. Maybe a Chinese with robbery in mind, or another Marine upset over someone messing with his poon-tang. There was a lot of jealousy over the Chinese girls, even the whores.

* * * * * *

We could sleep in as late as we wanted to after running the night jeep patrol and not getting to bed until 0100 or so. Our heat in the buildings was coal stoves and the mornings were beginning to get nippy. There were three of us NCOs in our hut. Casey and I and Sgt. Chenko, who pulled Sergeant of the Guard every fourth day. We had a Chinese boy, Number One Boys, as we called them, who took care of our hut and, not being too impressed with his Chinese name, we renamed him Lee. Lee was about fourteen years old. He would come in about daylight and while we snoozed away, he would build a fire in our cast iron stove and carry on with his other duties. We were cautioned by Capt. Pollard not to pay Lee more than fifty cents a week, as this was the accepted rate paid to all the Number One Boys and was really a lot of money for them.

The money exchange rate between American and Chinese money fluctuated between 3,000 to 1 and 6,000 to 1. Five dollars American would get you about 25,000 Chinese dollars, more or less, and a seven-course meal would cost no more than 3,000 dollars Chinese.

13

We had Lee do most of our shopping for us to avoid the haggling over price that was expected on any purchase. Our biggest expense item was light bulbs. The Chinese bulbs were all clear glass with a primitive looking element and if one light bulb lasted an entire evening, it was considered an old timer. Usually they blew out in five to thirty minutes. We had Lee buy them twenty at a time at fifteen cents each. The light bulbs were costing us more than Lee was.

At first, we had Lee do our laundry but as winter approached this outside task rendered his hands blue with cold and we began to seek another solution. All of the officers and some of the other Marines had already engaged the services of a Chinese laundryman who came every other day to pick up and deliver. He was a very sharp man and always carried an abacus with him. He could push those beads around faster than the eye could follow and come up with a mathematical solution in a twinkling. He spoke fluent English as well as French and I decided to learn spoken Chinese with his help. Each day he would spend a half hour or so with me and I would write down Chinese words as they sounded to the ear and memorize them. Within a month I could carry on a halting conversation in Chinese and continued to build my vocabulary. This was a great help to Casey and me on the patrol, although Casey refused to learn so much as one word of the "gook language" as he called it.

* * * * * *

We patrolled the whore houses of which there were three in Tangku. If trouble was in the air, that was usually where it started. A drunk Marine in a Chinese whore house is definitely trouble on the way to happen, especially when there are some Sailors scattered in.

Two of the houses didn't amount to a great deal and probably eighty percent of the business was conducted in the other. The old Chinese woman who ran it was all business. She had the most girls and the best-looking girls. She had fifteen girls when we first started the patrol and occasionally added another. Most of them were very young. When the Marines came in, she would line the girls up and the Marines would walk down the line and make a choice. Something like choosing pork chops in a meat market. The girls wore kimonos with nothing underneath and it was expected that the prospective customer would pull the kimono open to see if the inside was as attractive as the outside. There were a number of little cubby holes in the front of the house and in each there was a thin mattress and a blanket and pillow. This was where the entertainment went on.

In the back of the place was the old woman's living quarters. Her husband, an ageless Chinese who might have been forty or sixty, spent all of his time there. I never saw him out front. He had a round table no more than twelve inches off the floor and he sat beside it on a cushion and sipped hot wine. He had a small burner in the center of the table and heated the wine in a small brass kettle and then poured it into a brass cup from which he sipped.

He had a long drawn out Chinese name and the only part I could really pick up was "Ching" and that was what I called him. Ching was very fat and looked like a Buddha statue except that he always wore a hat reminiscent of the 30's, similar to those worn in a James Cagney movie. I never saw him without it. He was astounded the first time I spoke to him in Chinese and immediately invited me to share the hot wine with him. I accepted the offer and he got out another brass cup and I spent a lot of time at that table during my off hours.

* * * * * *

One-night, Casey and I were patrolling along the river and Casey said, "Something!" He pointed to our left and I backed up and shined our headlights over that way. There was a Chinese woman squatted on the bank of the river on a blanket. Casey said, "She's taking a crap."

I said, "Casey, have you ever seen a baby born?"

He said, "No, have you?"

"Not until now," I told him. She paid no attention to us and went on with her task which was well advanced. Finally, the baby slipped out on the blanket and she picked it up. It was a girl. We were that close. She cut the cord and held the baby up to the light while she stroked its forehead and inspected its feet and hands. Then she stood up and grasped the baby's feet in one hand and turned it upside down. She swung it twice to get momentum and threw it into the river. Casey leaped from the jeep. "My God! That baby was alive!"

I said, "Casey, get back in the jeep." My voice was thick with shock. Casey climbed back in and I shoved the jeep in gear and drove away from there fast.

* * * * * *

One night we checked the two houses that did the least of the business and it was quiet there. In one of them a Sailor had a girl on his lap and she was

15

feeding him something out of a bowl. The other house was deserted so we went on over to the action spot and went in. It was a little early for the real action, but the old woman had the girls lined up and right away I spotted a new girl. She was very small and had enough makeup on to make me suspicious. I walked over and opened her kimono with the billy club. She had neither breasts nor pubic hair. I thought, what the hell is this and I turned to the old woman. I could tell she was frightened, probably from the look on my face. In Chinese I said, "How old is that girl?"

"Shur-leo." Sixteen.

Like hell. I laid the club on the girl's shoulder and asked her how old she was. "Shur-ee."

Eleven. That I could believe. Her eyes were burning with resentment. I backed that old woman against the wall with the point of the stick. "If I ever catch that girl working here, I'll close you down!" I probably couldn't have closed down a flea circus, but she wasn't sure. "She wants to work," she said. "She begged me."

"If she wants to work, let her work in the kitchen or pack water for your other girls. No more working up here."

"She's broke in," she said in a low voice.

"Who broke her in?" I already knew. She dipped her head towards the back of the house. Her husband, Ching! The thought of that fat Chinaman with this eleven-year-old girl made me sick. I turned hot and then cold. I felt like going back there and killing him.

The old woman said desperately, "Ching wants you to come have wine with him."

I couldn't speak for a moment and then I said, "Tell him to go to hell." I had never been so enraged. Casey laid a restraining hand on my arm. "Let's get out of here," he said. We went out and climbed in the jeep. I was too upset to drive and traded places with Casey.

I mulled it around in my mind the next few days and I thought, "Who the hell am I to come over here and tell these people how to run their lives and their society?" I wasn't backing down, but I was trying to rationalize what was happening; maybe what had always happened.

16

After about a week, I cooled down and went back to see Ching. I couldn't help but like the old bastard. Maybe the way you would like Jesse James if he were to come back today. Or Butch Cassidy, or perhaps even Genghis Kahn. He was glad to see me, I could tell. He got out my cup and poured the wine. It was very hot and slipped down my throat like velvet. I forgave him, I guess.

* * * * * *

The old woman had one girl who was a favorite with most of the Marines and Sailors. Her features were a little different than most of the girls, maybe more of a Caucasian look, and the word spread that she was half White Russian. This was not true but it enhanced her appeal, for most of the servicemen were really eating their hearts out for a real American girl. The customers usually chose her if she was available and there were several fights over her. They had started calling her "Susie" and most of the Marines in Tangku knew who Susie was. Her Chinese nickname was "La Wo," which really means "number five," and indicated that she was the fifth child born in her family. She was a big drawing card for the old woman and received a certain amount of preferential treatment because of it.

One of her most devoted customers was a Sailor, a corpsman, who worked in the Navy hospital. He became obsessed with her and made the mistake of wanting her all to himself. This was out of the question, of course, but he persisted. He was really a decent fellow and I became fairly well acquainted with him. He had blond straw-colored hair and was rather short and a little on the heavy side. He seemed to have more money than most of the Americans and wasn't reluctant about spending it, especially on Susie. His name was Carstairs.

One thing that was allowed, indeed encouraged, was for the Marines and Sailors to walk the girls downtown and buy them things that struck their fancy, especially new clothes. The advantages of this to the girls and to the old woman were obvious. These girls had been sold to the old woman by their parents for sums of money, very little money usually, and they were bonded by contract to the old woman. Somewhere in fantasy was the belief that they were paying off their indebtedness and would someday be free. This, of course, never happened unless they became too old to be attractive any longer. If a girl became persistent in the idea of being freed from her contract, the old woman would present her with a new kimono, or a new blanket or pillow and this would thrust the girl back into debt from which she couldn't possibly recover.

Carstairs wanted to escort Susie downtown nearly every day to keep her away from the other servicemen. The old woman had few objections because Carstairs pressed dollar bills into her hand at frequent intervals. When Carstairs was on duty at the hospital, the old woman worked Susie in great haste to make up for any possible lost time. I kept thinking, "No good can come from this situation."

* * * * * *

There was a night club in Tangku and the Marines had dubbed it "The Coconut Grove." It was a sleazy place and had a Chinese band that did their best to play American songs to please the Marines and Sailors. They were out of tune most of the time but after a few drinks no one cared.

Casey and I kept a close eye on The Coconut Grove because if trouble spilled over out of the houses, this was where it collected. One night after checking the houses we pulled up in front of The Coconut Grove and we knew right away that something was wrong inside. The music wasn't playing and there was a great deal of noise that sounded like maybe two or three elephants tromping through a room full of pots and pans. Casey hit the deck running and I followed him in. A mighty big Marine was standing in the middle of the bandstand stomping drums and any other musical instrument that was unfortunate enough to come under his feet. Some twenty Chinese were attempting to halt the destruction with little or no success. The big Marine was picking them up and bouncing them bodily off the wall or off the floor. Casey whistled through his teeth. "He's a mean one," he said.

"We're meaner," I assured him. I made sure I had a good grip on the billy and stepped up on the bandstand. He blinked when he saw me. The sight of an MP brassard usually causes enough hesitation to give you an edge if you take advantage of it. I put the point of the billy in his chest and shoved. Casey placed his leg strategically behind the big Marine and he fell like a tree. I pinned him to the deck with the billy and stepped on his arm. Casey had the handcuffs on him before he knew what had happened. He was as gentle as a lamb after that. Casey looked at me and grinned. We were good at what we did.

18

We assisted him in the jeep and delivered him to Sgt. Chenko at the compound. "What's this all about?" demanded Chenko. "Aggravated cruelty," said Casey, smiling.

"Cruelty to who?"

"Twenty Chinese at The Coconut Grove."

"Okay. That's your joke for the day. Now tell me what happened." We did and made out our report. Chenko hollered at a couple of on-duty Marines in the back room and they came back and hauled the big Marine off to the brig.

* * * * * *

Lee had begun to get too big for his britches. It was probably a lot our own fault for spoiling him as much as we did. He started arriving later and going home earlier and doing as little as possible in the interim. One day he told me that he wanted to take three days off to visit his uncle in Tientsin. I agreed at once because I wanted to think about what to do.

The next morning, I went to the main gate and looked over the hundred or so Chinese who gathered there from sunup to sundown each day in case something might happen that would benefit them. It was seldom that anything did.

One little Chinese boy caught my eye. He stood with his mother and his clothes, while old, were clean and neatly patched. His face shown with cleanliness. I motioned for him to approach me and he did. He was quite small, hardly half as large as Lee. I told him what I had in mind and a smile broke across his face and he tapped his chest. "Me Number One Boy," he said in English.

Sgt. Chenko took a dim view of our new boy because of his size. "I doubt if he can carry a bucket of coal," he said.

"Then he can carry a half bucket at a time," I replied. The boy told me his name and I didn't care much for it, so we decided to call him "Joe." This pleased him. I think it gave him a sense of belonging to us.

* * * * * *

That night we ran out of light bulbs. I had forgotten to have Lee lay in a supply. No mind, I would get some tomorrow. I knew where the store was but had never been there. The next day about noon I drove over there. It was a dark and dingy place with a bowing Chinese man in attendance. The walls were lined with shelves loaded with items mostly beyond my identification. Rice and some other grains were presented in barrels sitting on the floor. One entire shelf was filled with boxes of tea. Stacks of candles were here and there, and I found the light bulbs piled loosely in a large cardboard box. He picked out twenty bulbs and put them in a cloth bag I had brought with me. As I was paying him, the entrance bell on the front door rang. A woman came in and I caught my breath. It had been a long time since I had seen a woman like this. I thought she must be a White Russian. The Chinese shopkeeper obviously knew her and followed her about the store, bowing constantly. She spoke to him in Chinese and her Chinese was much better than mine. She wished to go past me in the isle where I was standing and said, "Excuse me, please." I was struck with her accent. This was no White Russian: more likely British. I had made my purchase but was reluctant to leave.

She had brought a number of small silk bags with her and her purchases were put into these. Finally, she was ready to pay for everything and this placed her almost at my side. She smiled and said, "Hello there. You are one of the Marines." She was a striking woman. Her hair was dark with a hint of auburn and her eyes were dark although I couldn't actually tell their color. She was slender, like a willow, as they say. I felt a stirring in my groin and a shiver ran up my spine. She was a little older than I but I judged her as no more than thirty.

I offered to give her a lift as I had brought the jeep, but she smiled and declined. I went out and got in the jeep. It was late in November and it was quite cold with two or three inches of snow on the ground. I was still sitting there when she came out and I nodded as if to say, "Last chance." She laughed and without further hesitation got in beside me. I could hardly breathe, that was the way she affected me. She directed me which way to drive and we arrived at some common looking buildings about three blocks away.

Her apartment was upstairs, and she allowed me to help her with the supplies. Inside was like another world. The walls were completely covered with exquisite silk prints of Chinese scenes and her decorating motif was red

20

and black with splashes of gold here and there. There were no chairs, only cushions on the floor and two low tables like Ching's. She invited me to be seated and she disappeared behind a curtain into another room. When she came back, she had changed her street dress into a kimono, and she was very beautiful. She said, "Would you care for some tea?" I would and said so. She left again, behind another curtain, and reappeared with a teapot and two cups on a tray. The cups were thin and tiny and probably most expensive. I almost expected them to float away in the air like pretty bubbles.

She poured the tea, green in appearance, and took cream and sugar. I took neither. We talked for a long time but finally the spell was broken when I looked at my watch for I was due for jeep patrol in a half hour. She saw me to the door and as I stood there drinking in the sight of her, I had a strong feeling that there was a stirring in her groin also. I felt that I must have some kind of future with this woman. I said, "Could I see you again?" and she said, "Of course." We left it at that.

* * * * * *

When I got in the jeep, I brought forward a thought that had been in the back of my mind since I had bought the light bulbs. Something didn't add up. Either the shopkeeper had undercharged me, which was unlikely, or there was something rotten in Denmark. I drove back to the shop and went in.

"How much were the light bulbs?"

"Seven cents each."

"They were seven cents, not fifteen?"

"Ah, yes."

"Had they ever been fifteen cents?"

"Never."

Lee had been getting to us. He was making a neat profit of eight cents on each bulb. I had been feeling guilty and harboring a soft spot in my heart for Lee but now it faded away like fog from the river. I would make sure no one in the compound rehired him.

* * * * * *

21

Occasionally Casey and I patrolled up the river for a mile or so. We weren't really expected to but sometimes it helped to break the monotony. There were shacks here and there along the way built mostly from rough boards or even sticks and covered on the outside with mud. People actually lived in these hovels. Tonight, we were bouncing over the potholes when Casey said, "Something!" A hut was on fire. Three Chinese women were standing outside wringing their hands. I stopped the jeep and ran over and looked in the open space that served as a window. The inside was an inferno. Then I saw something moving, fluttering might be a better word, and it was a very old Chinese woman caught up in the flames. He hair was burned off and her clothes were on fire. Her eyes were rolled back in her head and her mouth was open, but no sound came out. Casey was looking over my shoulder and he said, "Christ almighty!" He pulled his .45 from the holster, jacked a cartridge into the chamber, stepped to the window and shot her in the face. The three women had collapsed and were beating their heads against the ground. One of them had tiny feet that had been bound when she was a baby to prevent their growth. It had been considered a genteel thing in the past but had just about died out in the present-day China. I could see Casey's face in the light from the fire and I didn't like what I saw. He was as white as the snow on the ground. I said, "Let's go, Casey." I backed the jeep around, and we drove back to Tangku.

* * * * * *

When Casey and I pulled up to the old woman's place the next night, she met us outside. She had never done that before. She was clearly upset. I finally got her slowed down to where I could understand her. Susie was gone. "Gone where?" She didn't know. She had left with Carstairs early in the day to go shopping and the old woman hadn't seen either of them since. The girls were always supposed to be back by 1700. I smelled a rat. I told her I would find out about it. We drove over to the hospital but Carstairs wasn't there. I learned he had taken an apartment and had been spending some time there recently.

We finished out the patrol and hit the sack. The next morning, I didn't have to hunt for Carstairs. He came to the compound to see me. Yes, he had Susie. He had decided to buy her from the old woman and release her from her bondage. I said, "Carstairs, you have to be out of your mind. The old woman will never let her go."

"I will offer her so much money she can't turn it down."

22

"What kind of money are you talking about? Susie's worth a thousand dollars a month to her in that house."

Carstairs thought for a minute. "My folks are very well to do, to put it mildly. I don't have the money now, but I can send for it and have it in ten days. What do you suggest I offer her?"

"I'm not suggesting anything. I think you are way off base and should bring her back and forget the whole thing."

"I won't do that. What if I offered her $2,000?"

"Carstairs," I said, "wise up. If you've got $2,000 to spend on a whore, why not take it a dollar at a time just like you've been doing?"

Carstairs said, "I'm not doing it for me. In fact, I just got the word that I'm being sent back to the States sometime in the next six seeks. I want Susie to be free and independent when I leave."

I said, "Carstairs, you are dreaming. There is no such thing as an independent whore in China."

He flinched. "She won't be a whore any longer, don't you see?"

I took a deep breath and blew it out. "What is it you want me to do?"

"You speak the lingo. I want you to go over there and negotiate with me. Tell the old woman I will have the money in less than two weeks."

"I don't think she will accept it," I said.

"I've got Susie," he reminded me.

I told him I would see what I could do. I drove over about noon and told the old woman of the developments. She didn't want the money; she wanted Susie. I finally made her see that she wasn't in much of a bargaining position and she said she would think about it.

That night on patrol, Carstairs flagged us down. Susie wanted to see me. Carstairs got in the jeep and we drove over to his apartment and went inside. Susie was there and Carstairs had bought a room full of stuff to make her comfortable and happy. Susie began to talk to me in Chinese and I gathered that she was concerned about her contract. It had been made up when she was sold and was signed by her parents and kept by the old woman to prove her

23

ownership. She must have the contract or Carstairs buying her back would mean nothing. I told her not to worry about it. I would make sure I got the contract.

* * * * * *

I waited for about a week before I went back to see the woman I had met at the shop. She let me in when I knocked, and I sat down on a cushion. I said, "I feel really dumb, but I don't even know your name." I told her my name, which is Lash. I learned not only her name that day but several more things about her. I had been way off in my geography but hadn't done badly on the accent. She was from South Africa and her name was Patricia Ashley-Brent. A tongue twister if I ever heard one. Her father had made a fortune manipulating mining stocks and making some investments in Johannesburg as well as some other areas. When he died in 1935, she had inherited everything. Her father had attempted to prepare her for this and sent her to exclusive schools in England and later to Paris, France; not really because South Africa didn't have some fine schools of their own, she said, but to give her a glimpse of the world other than South Africa and also because he could afford it.

It was a cruel blow to Pat when her father died. She was three when her mother died, and she had grown up adoring her father. Now she was thrust into a position she detested. She was expected to entertain and move about in a circle of society that had no appeal or meaning to her. She struggled through it for four years and then made arrangements with her attorney in Johannesburg to look after all her interests and she took a steamship cruise around the world. China fascinated her and when the tour was over, she returned and had been here ever since. Only her attorney knew where she was, and he posted a check to her bank in Tientsin every month. Pat liked China. She liked the people; she liked the solitude and the feeling that she was obligated to no one here. Her story made mine look pale by comparison, so I didn't dwell on it at all. She had left out one thing and I had to ask.

"Have you been married?"

"Never."

"Boyfriends?"

She smiled at me. "Of course. But never here in China."

I was perfectly at ease with her that day and I didn't want to wait any longer. I sat beside her and tipping her head back, I kissed her on the mouth. She responded deliciously and when I held her, she whispered, "Please hurry. It's been a long time for me." When I finally left her that evening, I felt that it had indeed been a long time for her. She nearly smothered me.

* * * * * *

The next morning, I woke up when Joe started building a fire in the stove and when I peeked out from under the covers, I saw Lee standing by the door watching every move Joe made. His three days had stretched into something more like two weeks. He was clearly concerned and when the room began to warm up, I thought, "What the hell," and I sat up on the side of the bed. Lee pointed at Joe and said, "Two Number One Boys?" I said, "No, Lee. One Number One Boy," and I indicated Joe. Lee was hurt. I stood up and pointed to the light bulb in the center of the ceiling. "Light bulbs do not cost fifteen cents, Lee." If you can say Chinese flush, Lee certainly did. He couldn't speak. I said, "Give me your pass, Lee." It was a typewritten card prepared in the Officer on Duty's office and without it no Chinese could enter the compound. He produced it from somewhere in his padded clothes and I tore it across and across again and dropped it in the stove. It would be something like if someone tore up your Social Security Card and you could never, ever, get one again; only worse.

Chenko sat up and said, "That was a shitty thing to do."

I said, "Mind your own business, Chenko."

Casey said nothing. To him all Chinese were "gooks" and not worthy of any particular attention. Lee left and I got up and watched him until he disappeared through the main gate. I'll have to admit that I felt some pain over the whole situation.

* * * * * *

Something was going on in the compound that I didn't like. Capt. Pollard had started bringing a Chinese girl into the compound at night and letting her go home at daylight. This appealed to some of the other officers and NCOs and several of them started bringing in their own girls. The rank and file thought it was a capital idea and the whole thing went from bad to worse. Even Chenko went for the idea but Casey and I put our foot down on that. We had enough of that sort of thing on the patrol without bringing it into our own living quarters.

Capt. Pollard was not a good officer or even a good Marine in my opinion. Somewhere along the line he had made a wrong turn and got mixed up in the Marines and he was out of his element. It was something we would have to live with.

* * * * * *

Big ships cannot come into shore at Tangku. The rivers over the centuries have carried mud and debris into the Yellow Sea until, close to shore it is too shallow for anything but small craft barges. The Yellow Sea gets its name from the yellow mud that is not far beneath the surface. The big ships must anchor twenty to forty miles out depending on the depth they draw. However, there is much activity at the docks, and barges towed by tugs are constantly bringing in supplies from the ships out there. Navy launches are much in evidence bringing in American Sailors and officers for liberty and other business or activity. Casey and I would drive along the docks from time to time just to see what was going on. One evening just after we started patrol, a Navy launch came in and I was startled to see Capt. Pollard step out on the dock. The coxswain helped him manhandle a large cardboard carton from the launch to the dock. It was past dark, and Capt. Pollard didn't see us. He began to shout, "Rickshaw, rickshaw!" of which there were usually plenty around. He was surrounded by three in a flash and after making his choice, he wrestled the box onto the seat and crawled in beside it. We followed at a discreet distance and he led us to a broken-down area that we usually avoided. The rickshaw stopped and I parked the jeep and left Casey to guard it while I checked out what was going on. Capt. Pollard got out and knocked on a door and when it opened, two Chinese men came out and got the carton and carried it inside. A few minutes later, Capt. Pollard came out, got in the rickshaw and disappeared into the darkness.

I went back to the jeep and I told Casey, "I think Capt. Pollard is in the black-market business." The carton was probably cigarettes. It was well known that their black-market potential was lucrative. We paid fifty cents a carton for cigarettes and on the streets, they would bring $3.50 to $5.00 American. Luckies and Camels were worth $5.00 while Chesterfields and Old Golds brought $3.50. For this reason, they were rationed to us at one carton per week for each man. If you were broke, but could come up with a carton of cigarettes, you could go on a very good liberty. It happened all the time, but a case at a time is something else. We decided to forget that we had seen anything.

* * * * * *

I had been back to see Pat twice more and then got Casey to cover for me and started spending some of my nights there. This was no problem, as Capt. Pollard was so wrapped up in his own goals that discipline was pretty much a thing of the past. I even picked her up in the jeep a few times and we drove into the countryside, bundled against the cold and sipping tea from a thermos she brought along. Pat enjoyed this as much as I did as she had no transportation other than rickshaws or the train on her infrequent trips to Tientsin or Peiping. It would have been nicer in the summer but we both realized, though we never mentioned it, that I probably wouldn't be there when summer came again.

One day we drove out northwest of Tangku and I saw hundreds of crude wooden boxes in a field and started over there for a closer look. Pat said, "Don't go near them," and then she told me what they were…coffins. When the people died in the winter, the ground was frozen and grave digging was suspended. In the spring and summer when it thawed out again, the burial was completed, maybe.

Pat had started calling me "Pico" and I had no idea why. At first, I felt a resentment about it but when we were lying under the covers at night and she would whisper "Pico" in my ear any objections I might have had faded into the darkness. I did ask her if one of her old boyfriends was named Pico and she said certainly not. It was a special name she had for me. I accepted this but I have always been a guy who never really trusted a woman and sometimes I even had reservations about Pat.

* * * * * *

One morning before I was out of bed, Carstairs came to the compound. He had the money and wanted to get on with buying Susie. I went with him and Susie insisted that we have the contract before we delivered the money. I left them and took the money, all in one hundred-dollar bills, and drove over to the old woman's house. I told her I was ready to pay her and pick up the contract. She told me to wait and she went into the back room. She was gone so long I walked back and peeked through the curtain. She was talking in a low voice to Ching. I was already sick of the whole situation but decided to

27

go on with it after coming this far. When she came out, she said they couldn't find the contract, but they would look for it and they would have it tomorrow. It was something I had no choice but to accept so I went back and told Carstairs about it. He said, "Okay. Tomorrow it is then." I made him take the money back. I certainly didn't want to be responsible for it overnight.

The next day I picked up the money again and drove over to the old woman's house. She had the contract. It was on a heavy piece of white paper something like butcher's paper and was tied with a piece of silk cloth. I opened it up. It was about two feet long and maybe eighteen inches wide. It was covered with Chinese characters and meant nothing to me. I studied it as though I knew what I was doing and finally gave her the $2000. I was relieved to be done with it. I drove back over to the apartment and gave the scroll to Carstairs. He opened it upon a low table and Susie darted to his side to see for herself. She immediately went into a fit of moaning and throwing herself about. She was crying. It was the wrong paper…it was a forgery. I could see Ching and that old woman sitting up all night to copy it off the original. They had the money and we had a piece of paper worth nothing.

I told Carstairs, "Don't worry. I am fed up. I'll see you in an hour." I drove back to the compound and got my MP brassard and billy club and buckled on my .45. This always impressed the Chinese and I was tired of messing around. The old woman saw me when I came in the door and she guessed what I was there for. I put the point of the billy in her chest and said, "I want that contract and I want it now."

She backed away saying, "Yes, yes, yes," in Chinese. The charade was over. She went into the back room and reappeared at once with another scroll similar in appearance to the forgery. I didn't bother to open it. I knew this was the original contract.

* * * * * *

I had no regrets about my choice of Number One Boys when I hired Joe. He was nine years old and was far wiser than his years. He performed his duties with dispatch and care. Our billet was spotlessly clean, and Joe spent a great deal of time keeping it that way. Even Sgt. Chenko admitted that we had made a wise choice.

Joe made it known to me one day that if he were allowed to purchase a small kerosene burner that he could prepare some Chinese delicacies for us.

28

It sounded like a good idea to me and I gave him some money and he trotted off to return with a little stove, three small pans, and an assortment of foods ready for his preparation. When I questioned him about it, he told me that his mother had taught him much about cooking. Joe was a rarity among Chinese children; he was an only child. His father, he told me, had been killed…drowned, he thought, before he was born. He was close to his mother and she walked with him to the compound every morning and returned to accompany him home at night. Their baggy, quilted clothes were always clean and neatly patched. His mother had the most patient face I saw in all of China. It was obvious that she adored her only son.

Joe's culinary arts produced what would have to be called hors d'oeuvres rather than anything like a main dish. He would fry little thin pancakes and then fill them with preparations of his own manufacture and rolled like a tortilla. They were delicious. While we ate them, he would sit and watch us with great delight. I grew to have a great deal of respect and compassion for Joe.

* * * * * *

Pat had decided that we should go to Peiping for a holiday, as she called it. She had been there before, of course, and was anxious for me to see the ancient city with her. It took some doing but I managed to get a ten-day pass and Casey arranged to run the patrol with the assistance of a corporal named Barnett.

We went on the train, of course, as there was certainly no other way to travel. When we crept through the outskirts of Tientsin, I was struck with the reality of the war that was smoldering in this vast nation. Machine guns were set up on all the roads leading out of the city and Chinese Nationalist soldiers in their drab uniforms hunkered behind sandbag barricades playing ancient gambling games and smoking countless cigarettes. It was bitter cold in our train car, and we had worn our heaviest clothing and coats. All the glass was gone from the windows having been shot out by the Chinese Reds when the train went through their area on the way to Peiping. We got a firsthand taste of this when the conductor came through shouting in Chinese for everyone to lie on the floor as we were about to pass through a cut in the hills from which the Reds always fired at the train. They did not disappoint us this time and the bullets whipped over our heads and thudded into the walls with great ferocity. I put my arm across Pat's back, and I could feel her trembling.

When we finally arrived in Peiping, I was struck with the milling activity. Rickshaws seemed to be everywhere, and throngs of Chinese scurried about like ants, each apparently bent on their own pursuits. Directly before us as we stepped off the train was a huge structure towering some four or five hundred feet into the air with a two-story picture of Chang Kai-Shek in the center. Pat said it Chine Men Tower, the middle gate to Inner City. We engaged three rickshaws, one for each of us and another to transport our luggage, and Pat gave directions that would take us to a hotel of her choice and where she always stayed when in Peiping.

I had been surprised when I first arrived in China to learn that the North Chinese people had no knowledge of the term "rickshaw." They caught on fast enough when the Marines insisted on shouting "rickshaw" but their own term for those conveyances was "jo-pee." If there happened to be a temporary shortage of available rickshaws, which sometimes happened as curfew approached, I could shout "jo-pee" above all the Marine voices calling for rickshaws and would have one at my side at once.

We arrived at a large sprawling building enclosed with a high stone fence and a Chinese guard, a policeman apparently, posted at a gate to keep multitudes of Chinese people from entering. I didn't see any indication in English of the buildings' identity, but Pat said she thought it was the former Italian Embassy and was now a luxurious hotel with several cafes and two bars. Our room was spacious with thick carpeting on the floor and the bathroom was decorated with pale pink inlaid tile from floor to ceiling.

After unpacking, we lay on the bed together and she stroked my back with her cool long fingers. I could have spent the entire ten days right in this room without any regrets. After a leisurely hot bath together, we had lunch brought up to our room rather than leave its sanctuary now. I should make it clear at once that Pat was paying the bill for this trip. A Marine sergeant's pay would not have carried us very far, not even in Peiping. I didn't let it bother me as there was no other way and we were too close to each other now to worry about trivialities like money.

* * * * * *

We enjoyed a late breakfast the next morning and decided to engage a motor car for our convenience the rest of our stay in Peiping. This we did through the hotel and were blessed with an American-made Ford sedan

30

manufactured in 1936. It was in surprisingly good condition and even had a working heater. Our chauffeur was a remarkable Chinese man perhaps thirty years old who apparently knew Peiping as well as the back of his hand and spent most of his time bowing and blinking his eyes at us. We called him Hwang Ho, which seemed to meet with his approval. This first day we decided to visit the Chinese bazaars of which there were several in Peiping. They were fantastic structures, some three or four stories high and there are literally hundreds of small individual shops inside; something like booths at a fair. If they don't have what you want in a Chinese bazaar, you don't need it. Pat wanted to buy some more Chinese silk prints similar to the ones on her apartment walls and we located a luggage shop where we purchased a suitcase to carry them in. She selected a bag of excellent construction and made entirely of fine heavy leather with straps and a stout locking mechanism. After a great deal of bargaining during which the shopkeeper assured us constantly that he was losing money, she finally purchased it for $8.00 American.

We spent perhaps two hours in a glass shop that had the most exquisite colored glass figurines and novelties that can be imagined. There were tiny dragons, no more than three inches long so delicately fashioned as to seem unreal. Pat bought some glass objects that caught her fancy and they were carefully enclosed in cotton and placed in the suitcase.

Back at the hotel that evening we bathed and changed in our room and lay on the bed for an hour or so to admire each other. When we entered the dining room, I had two one-dollar bills folded in my hand to assure that the maître d would show us to a good table, and he did. In the better Chinese nightclubs, it is never necessary to snap your fingers for a waiter. Your waiter is assigned to you and you alone. He is constantly at your table awaiting your pleasure. Pat wanted to have Peiping duck as I had never enjoyed this famous dish. We placed our order and ordered a bottle of wine. Shortly, a Chinese man appeared carrying four dressed ducks for our selection. We were to choose our duck after which it would be returned to the kitchen and roasted. To me they all looked alike, but I selected a likely looking fellow that would soon be our main course. During the next hour so many dishes of delicacies were set before us that I actually lost count, but there were more than twenty. Some things, such as tiny shrimp and bean sprouts, I could identify but the majority were unknown to me, although everything was delicious. We forced ourselves to be conservative in order to do justice to the main courses. We used chopsticks as was expected and Pat was quite good with them. Our waiter had wisely set a spoon and fork at the side of my plate or I might have starved to death. When they brought our duck, done to a turn, I was first expected to give my approval of its appearance, which I did and then our waiter produced a carving knife that must have been sharper than a razor. With rapier fast strokes, almost faster than the eye could follow, he cut scores of tiny pieces of meat and we wrapped them in wheat pancakes with a sauce and strips of radish and onion. We rolled them like tortillas, reminiscent of Joe's efforts, and my initiation to Peiping Duck was a very pleasant experience.

* * * * * *

After two days in the bazaars, we were ready to tour the Forbidden City. This is the innermost of four cities, one within the other, which make up Peiping. Chinese is the outer city, then Tarter, followed by Imperial City and finally Forbidden City in the center. The Forbidden City is entered through an edifice called the Gate of Heavenly Peace and this, too, carried a huge picture of Chiang Kai-Shek. It would be impossible to tour the Forbidden City in one day and see even a fraction of the treasures there. We spent several hours in the Audience Hall which was now a museum. There were treasures beyond imagination. At one point we admired a solid gold Buddha enclosed in glass and guarded by Monks. There was a dragon carved from solid jade with ruby eyes that seemed to be watching us. Monks in long gold colored smocks were nearly everywhere. Usually they were kneeling and praying. Some were very old and others quite young, boys actually. On our way back to the hotel that afternoon we saw a camel train coming into the city and I was captivated by the wild appearance of the men. They were dressed entirely in clothes made of animal hides and furs and their features were decidedly different form the Chinese people of Peiping or Tientsin. Hwang Ho, our driver, said they were coming in from the Gobi Desert. We spent the next two days in the Forbidden City drinking in its treasures to be stored away in our memories.

One night the electricity was off over the entire city and the streets were black and spooky. Now I could understand why candles were so much in evidence everywhere. There were several in our room and we took advantage of what little light they gave.

Next, we decided to see the Summer Place located about eight miles from the city. It was constructed by the Empress Dowager between 1888 and 1893 and has some stunning Chinese structures such as the Marble Boat floating on a lake. It was built with taxes that had been raised to build a Chinese Navy.

We walked across the famous Camel Back Bridge and at one point entered a temple to admire a ferocious appearing statue of a Chinese god that must have stood some one hundred feet high. Buddhas and statues are everywhere in the temples. Literally thousands of them ranging in size from minute figures that could be held in the palm of one's hand to those one hundred feet or taller. We also visited an area known as the Western Hills before driving back to our hotel.

* * * * * *

Pat and I had fallen into the habit of stopping at the bar before entering the dining room for a drink and to admire the décor there which was European, Italian specifically, and seemed something of a relief from the overwhelming Chinese influence. This evening I left Pat alone briefly while I entered the hotel lobby to get a package of cigarettes. When I returned a Marine corporal, obviously a little under the influence, had taken over my stool and was attempting to engage Pat in conversation. She was doing her best to ignore him. I have never been the type who taps someone on the shoulder and says, "I say there, old boy," or something like that. Nearly eight years in the Marine Corps had molded me into a man who can make fast decisions and come up with the decisive action. I saw at once that most of the Marine's weight was on the bar stool, so I grasped the stool and yanked it from under him. Down he went but was up at once and charged me like a bull charging the cape. I feinted left, stepped right, and chopped him at the base of the neck. Instinctively I delivered the next blow which can kill a man, indeed, that is its purpose, but fortunately I had the presence of mind to pull the punch. Nevertheless, he crumpled like a steer in a slaughterhouse. He was out cold. I took Pat's arm and guided her from the room.

* * * * * *

We spent the next two days driving around under Hwang Ho's experienced guidance, admiring such treasured sights as Western Hills, the Loma Temple, the Whispering Wall, the beautiful Jade Fountain of Peiping and an area known as the Coal Hill. We drove for several hours through the streets of Peiping dotted with markets and Bazaars. The street names were fascinating. "Wang Tu Ching," "Tung Chian Min," Chung Wan Man," to name a few.

One morning we paused for a few minutes to watch a truck and a crew of Chinese picking up the week's dead. When the poor and the unfortunate die on the sidewalks, which happens frequently, they are rolled into the gutters

33

where they lie until the truck makes its weekly tour to pick them up. In one block while we watched, they picked up seven bodies and threw them haphazardly into the back of the truck.

* * * * * *

We had saved the Great Wall of China until last. It is located several miles to the north of Peiping at this point. We had a beautiful lunch prepared at the hotel kitchen to take with us. Enforced by a large thermos of hot tea we were prepared to spend the day and so we did.

The structure shocks the senses when you think of its immensity, its age, its purpose, and its durability. The Wall is entered through parapets located at about one-half mile intervals along its length and you climb stone steps to reach the top. Once there, you could drive an automobile along its surface. Designed to repel the barbarians from the North, the Great Wall stands as a monument to man's visions, to his fears, his aspirations, his weaknesses, his strengths, and most of all to his frailty and his briefness of time upon this earth. We stood close together, Pat and I, and saw the Great Wall dip and climb across the hills and finally to fade into the distance.

* * * * * *

My leave was up, and we must now return to Tangku. We boarded the train the next morning and the trip back was similar to the trip when we came to Peiping. The Chinese Reds faithfully peppered our car with rifle shot as we crept through the cut in the hills. I think they deliberately fired at the top of the cars in order not to hit anyone riding inside. Either that, or they were lousy marksmen.

When the train pulled into Tangku, we made arrangements with rickshaws to transport ourselves and our luggage to Pat's apartment. I elected to stay all night, as I was not to report back to duty until the following morning. It had been a leave I would never forget but it was good to be back in Tangku.

* * * * * *

Casey was glad to see me and I him. He didn't have the confidence in Corporal Barnett that existed between Casey and me. There had been one important development while I was gone. Capt. Pollard had gone too far and became careless with his cigarette transactions and a Navy officer accompanied by two Sailors had followed him. He was arrested while in the act of accepting

34

money for cigarettes and had been taken somewhere, probably Tientsin, for possible Court Martial.

Our new Commanding Officer was already in charge. His name was Capt. Jacoby and I liked him at once. He was strictly military, what the Marines call "spit and polish," and things were already clicking with military precision under his command. His last duty had been with the Fifth Marine Division and he had been on Iwo Jima where a burst from a Jap machine gun had nearly killed him. He had spent the next five months in a Navy hospital near San Francisco while they put him back together. He intended to be a career officer and had requested China duty. No longer were Chinese girls allowed in the compound at night and some of the Marines who had done little or nothing under Capt. Pollard's command found that there were any number of tasks to be performed and that they were better off to be busy once again.

* * * * * *

Carstairs was glad to see me. He was being sent back to the States in less than ten days and wanted to make some arrangements for Susie's benefit before he left. He could be really dumb at times and he proved it now by asking me if I would be interested in taking over Susie when he left. I said, "No thanks," and asked him what he had in mind. He wanted to put her on the train, give her some extra money and send her back to her parents who lived in a small town not far from Peiping. I thought this was a bad solution and told him so, but he was determined, and even Susie seemed anxious to see her family again. We went ahead with it and I drove them both to the train depot and waited around while Carstairs bought her ticket and stood with his arm around her while we waited for the train to leave. She embraced him with apparent passion at the last and boarded the train at the last moment.

I watched until it was lost from sight and when I turned around, Carstairs was sitting on the edge of the dock with his face hidden in his hands and his shoulders were shaking. I was struck by this show of emotion, but when he raised his face, I saw that he was convulsed by mirth, not sorrow. And then he told me, during that last hot embrace, Susie had lifted his wallet and his wristwatch.

* * * * * *

A few days later, Casey and I were patrolling near the train depot when we saw a crowd of Chinese, mostly children, clustered around something lying

35

on the ground near the tracks. We investigated and there was a small Chinese boy lying there with one arm across his face. The other arm was gone, and he was bleeding to death. These children would fight desperately for a piece of coal the size of a walnut and had apparently been so engaged when the train had moved unexpectedly, and the boy's arm had been severed just below the elbow. The small hand and lower arm still lie there. I knelt at his side and moved his arm from across this face and recoiled with shock. It was Joe, our Number One Boy! I shouted for Casey to bring the First Aid kit and applied a tourniquet to stop the flow of blood. He was pale as death. I picked him up in my arms, ran to the jeep and told Casey to drive to the Navy Hospital as fast as he knew how. I became aware that Joe was looking into my eyes and whispering something. I leaned forward and he was saying, "Wa ny nee." Literally translated it means "I love you," but has a much deeper meaning in Chinese. "Wa ny nee, Joe," I replied. When we got to the hospital I started in the door and Carstairs appeared and stood blocking my way. He said, "You can't bring that Chink in here." I said, "This is not a Chink. It is Joe, my Number One Boy." "You can't bring him in here," said Carstairs stubbornly.

I spoke very softly and made sure I didn't raise my voice. I said, "Carstairs, get out of my way or I will kill you."

I carried Joe back to a room that smelled of fresh paint and antiseptic and laid him on a table. A Navy doctor in khaki pants and white T-shirt appeared sipping a glass of some amber-colored fluid. "Well, now." He smiled showing me a mouth full of strong white teeth. "What have we here?" He set the glass down, walked over to a sink and started washing his hands. I walked out and sat down in the first chair I came to. Now that it was over, I felt like crying, so I did.

I went out and Casey was waiting in the jeep. "What about this?" said Casey and he indicated something in the back of the jeep. I looked and felt like screaming. It was Joe's hand and arm. Someone had thrown it in the jeep as we drove away. I didn't want to take it in the hospital and have them grind it up or burn it or whatever they do. To throw it in the river would be obscene. I thought about burying it, but the ground was frozen a foot deep everywhere. And then it came to me. I would bury it after all. I told Casey to drive back to the compound and I took the arm and went to our quarters. Sgt. Chenko was lying on his bed, a habit which had earned him the nickname of "blanket ass," and he sat up and peered over to see what I was doing. I laid Joe's arm down and went out to get a shovel. When I came back Sgt. Chenko was leaning over to see what I had laid on the floor and he staggered back and said, "What the hell is that?"

I said, "Shut up, Chenko," and started digging a hole in the dirt floor. Sgt. Chenko got back on his bunk, lay back and stared at the ceiling.

I dug a hole about a foot and a half deep and took Joe's arm and wrapped it in a piece of blanket I had torn off one of mine, placed it in the hole and covered it up again. Casey came in and told Chenko what had happened and Chenko didn't say another word to me. He knew better.

* * * * * *

I would spend as much time as I possibly could with Pat and came to feel that I had known her forever. There really wasn't much for us to do in Tangku except talk and make love. I didn't dare take her out at night, especially to a place like The Coconut Grove and she wouldn't have gone even if I had asked her. Sometimes when we were together, she seemed distant as though she had something on her mind that she couldn't, or wouldn't, share with me. But she seemed to love me deeply and I accepted her as she was.

I made it a point to visit Joe every day and he was recovering rapidly. He couldn't have been under better care if he had been Commander of the Pacific Fleet. The Navy doctors had trimmed the outraged bone and tissue of this severed arm and fashioned flaps of skin across the end and it was healing nicely. His mother had learned from me what had happened, and I engineered a plan that allowed her to visit him every few days. Also, I gave her money, as much as a dollar a week usually, and each time a tear would escape and slide down her cheek.

* * * * * *

One day on patrol we had driven to the north side of town and we saw a large crowd of Chinese milling about, something in their midst. I drove over to see what was going on and they had constructed a tripod of poles rising some twelve feet in the air and had hung someone by his hands in such a manner that his feet were a foot off the ground. Most of them carried sticks and as they moved about, they struck the hapless person with them and already his face was covered with blood. They were chanting a word in Chinese over and over and I suddenly caught its meaning. "Thief, thief, thief," they were saying.

Casey said, "This is nothing for us. Let's get out of here." I hesitated to leave. Something about the figure was familiar to me and as I drove closer, I knew who it was. It was Lee, our first Number One Boy. I told Casey, "I am going to get him out of there." This could be easier said than done and I turned the problem over in my mind. They clearly intended to kill him and if I were to do anything at all to help Lee, it would have to be done quickly. I had never drawn my .45 against the Chinese and to do to now would be viewed with alarm by our officers. I made my decision, drew the weapon and put a shell into the chamber. They were in an ugly mood and held their ground when I advanced. I drew a breath and fired over their heads. They fell back but only briefly, and I fired two more shots over their heads; lower this time and they moved away from the tripod. I cut Lee down and took him in my arms as he was unable to stand. Casey brought the jeep up and I climbed in and the Chinese mob surged forward prompting Casey to throw the jeep into reverse for some one hundred yards before turning around and driving us away from there.

I abandoned caution and instructed Casey to drive back to the compound where I took Lee into our quarters and assessed his injuries. All of his front teeth were gone which accounted for most of the blood, but otherwise we seemed to have rescued him in time. He would never win a corn on the cob eating contest, but he would live. I helped him clean up and I said, "Lee, if you really have an uncle in Tientsin, my advice to you is to go there." He agreed readily and we waited until it was nearly time for the train to depart. Casey and I drove him over there. I bought his ticket, gave him ten dollars American, and he was gone.

* * * * * *

Carstairs' orders came through and he told me goodbye at the hospital one day while I was there visiting Joe. He felt good about what he had done for Susie in spite of her breach of good conduct at the last. I had to admit that it had worked out well for her.

One cold windy morning I drove over to see Pat. I was alarmed when there was no answer to my knocking on the door. I couldn't imagine where she could be this early in the day. I went back down the steps and there was a Chinese man standing at the foot. I had seen him around before and presumed he must live somewhere nearby. I asked him in Chinese if he had seen Pat or knew where she might be. He assured me that he knew nothing. He remembered nothing, he was just a poor man trying to feed his wife and eight children. He was a humble man, he said, and was not worthy to even be in my presence. I soon tired of listening to this garbage and started walking back to the jeep. Then I heard him hissing deep in his throat, like a snake in a jar. I walked back until I stood in front of him. In my anxiety over Pat I had nearly forgotten the Chinese Cardinal Rule. I took out three one-dollar bills and handed them to him and his memory returned with abound. From somewhere in his dirty sleeve he brought out a red envelope with a black border of Chinese characters around its edge. I knew at once it was from Pat. I went back to the jeep, got in and opened the envelope. There was a single page inside, gold in color and edged in red. She had written her message in black ink and had apparently used a coarse pen that made her words stand out like Chinese characters:

Dearest Pico,

This is the most difficult decision that I have ever faced in my life. My love for you has passed beyond reason and I think of little else. I ask myself over and over, "What is to become of us?" Every time you come through the door, I hold my breath for fear that you will tell me you are being sent back to your United States. When you leave, I wonder if I will ever see you again. Because of this, I am not happy and contented here as I was before. I am in constant torment and I cannot live that way. Also, I am so worried about the war that is coming closer to us. I don't know what will happen to General Chiang Kai-Shek and his brave people.

I have decided, for your sake and mine, to go away for a time and get my thoughts straightened out. Please don't attempt to find me, as you could not. China is such a very large place and the world, of course, is even larger. I shall never stop loving you and I am enclosing the address of my attorney in Johannesburg so that if you wish you may someday contact me through him. Please do not be angry with me and try to understand why I am doing this.

My love forever,

Pat

I stared at the slip of paper with the attorney's address and very slowly crumpled it and made a ball between my thumb and forefinger. I flipped it away. I started the jeep and put it in gear. I never saw her again.

* * * * * *

On my next day off duty I decided to take the jeep and drive over and see Ching. When I walked in the front, I glanced at the girls seated here and there and there smiling at me was Susie. She was wearing a new blue kimono and the combs in her hair sparkled with glass beads. Her makeup was carefully applied, and I knew she was back in business. I sat down beside her and said, "Tell me about it, Susie."

She had ridden the train to the village where her parents lived and walked to her old home where she had been born and raised to puberty. Her heart leaped when she saw her mother bent over some task in the hut, but her mother drew back and would neither speak to her nor touch her. They both cried. Her brothers and sisters viewed her with curiosity and resentment and feared that she had returned to share their meager rations. She was about as welcome as a visit from a corpse. Her father was furious and demanded that she depart at once which she hastened to do.

She boarded the train again and rode as far as Tientsin, where she made her way to a place she had heard of called Roof Garden. It was a three-story structure covering nearly a square city block. Inside, circular hallways went around each floor with two room apartments opening on both sides. Since the arrival of the Marines, the Roof Garden had become a gigantic house of prostitution. Each two-room apartment was occupied by a Chinese family, sometimes a dozen or more including grandparents, parents, aunts and uncles, children and the young girls or women who supported everyone by their activities in the frontmost room.

Susie, who still had some of Carstairs' money left, bought a pillow and blanket and gained permission to share an apartment with a girl who was supporting fifteen members of her family. This arrangement soon lost favor when it became apparent that Susie's Caucasian appearance was getting her most of the customers and they confiscated her possessions, robbed her of her money, and turned her out of their door. New she was homesick, broke, and in despair and the thought of returning to the old woman became desirable to her. She worked the streets for two nights and made enough money to feed herself and buy a train ticket to Tangku.

I said, "Are you free then, Susie?"

"Very soon," she replied. "I signed a new contract for I had no pillow, no blanket and only one kimono. When I pay for those, then I will be free."

I said, "Susie, good luck. You are going to need it."

I felt very much like getting drunk and I went into the back room. Ching raised his hand in greeting, "Ding hao!"

I looked into Ching's eyes and I saw China there. I saw a billion Chinese marching forever. I saw patience beyond comprehension, there were solid gold statues and a mountain of jade and I saw time slowly unraveling like a ball of yarn and having neither beginning nor end. If I had had the time, I could have watched ten million Chinese building the Great Wall a stone at a time. It was all there in Ching's eyes. I stood up. I was drunk, alright.

When I got to the door I looked back and Ching seemed to be floating in the air, like a giant balloon. My eyes struggled to get him back down where he belonged. And then his face became very clear to me, like a full moon on a winter night. He was smiling.

I said, "Ching. You son of a bitch!"

I went out and got in the jeep and drove back to the compound.

The End

SECTION II

Makin Island Raid

At dawn on this date a U.S Submarine lay quietly off the shore of Japanese occupied Makin Island.

There were some 200 American Marines on the sub. They were inflating and launching a number of rubber boats in which to make their way to the island. It was still dark, and a certain amount of confusion was evident for the water was rough and churning about the hull of the listing sub.

However, a confident and inspiring voice came out of the darkness, and the confusion was defeated. The owner of that assuring voice was Marine Col. Evans F. Carlson, veteran officer and fighting man of many Chinese-Jap battles.

His order was brief and to the point, he said, "Follow me."

He was not the Commander who stays securely at the Command Post Base waiting for the success or failure of his men, he was gambling his life on the ability of those men to win.

At the Colonel's side was Marine Major James Roosevelt, son of the President himself, 2ⁿᵈ In command. The fighting spirit and confidence of those two great officers was echoed by every Devil-dog making their way through those shark-infested waters that morning.

As they neared the beach great breakers swept them at break-neck speed in this rubber craft toward the treacherous coral reefs.

Many of the motors with which each boat was equipped had long since ceased to run and were thrown overboard to be rid of all unnecessary weight.

As the boats struck the beach the Col. Leaped out upon the sand and began silently organizing his Company's.

Feeling sure the Japs were as yet unaware a raid was in evidence the Raiders began reconnoitering and making their way farther up the beach caching their boats.

Everything was in order for a surprise assault until someone accidently discharged a burst of fire from a B.A.R.

Knowing then that they were discovered the Raiders began making their way toward the Jap positions prepared to open fire at the first enemy movement.

The Island was small, about six miles long and a scant one-fourth mile wide. At one end the Japanese had made their headquarters and installations including barracks to house some 80 troops stationed there.

At the extreme other end of the Isle was a village of natives. Many had been tortured and ravished by the Japs, and still others had been murdered in cold blood. All the young men and women had long since been killed by the bloody Japs and of the 1700 yet remaining, all were very old or very young.

Upon learning that the Marines were intending to rid the Island of Japanese this good folk were overjoyed and did everything in their power to help the Devil-dogs.

While moving forward for their first attack however, the Marines had not yet contracted the help of these natives. Even then they were moving with great caution. The Japs surprised them suddenly with burst of machine gun fire directly in front and on both sides of the Marines. Hitting the deck and cursing between their teeth the Americans returned the assault with a fire so deadly the Japs were nearly silenced.

Deciding they had walked into the middle of a number of machine gun nests. Small numbers of Marines were sent out on both flanks to capture the Japanese positions.

A Corporal in charge of our party easily wiped out a Jap machine gun nest. Spotting two more he moved forward and with well-aimed hand grenades, completed wiping out a total of three Jap machine guns.

Moving forward once more with only light casualties, the Marines watched carefully on all sides for any indications of Jap snipers strapped in the foliage of coconut trees. As the Raiders came into range, they opened fire from their unseen positions causing the Marines to take cover and return the fire ten-fold.

While the Japs were armed with bolt action rifles. The Raiders possessed nothing but automatic weapons. Many Japs were skulking behind trees and picking out a man they would fire and duck behind trees and picking out a man they would fire and duck behind the tree until the Marine would fire.

Believing then he would also have to work his bolt, they would peer around the tree once more only to stop a well-aimed shot from the Marine M-1.

In the meanwhile, another group of the Raiders had become separated at the sub and instead of landing at the right place, had landed farther down the beach, behind the Japanese positions. Not knowing where they were at, nor where the rest of the outfit were, they opened fire on the Japs causing a great deal of consternation among those sun worshipers. Caught between two fires the Japanese became worried nearly to hysteria.

A group of Japs pouring from a barracks door were cut down as weeds before a hoe.

While the fighting was continuing thick and heavy, the Japanese sent out word by radio of their predicament and soon Jap Zero planes roared over dropping deadly cargoes of bombs, the Raiders, however, in their green dungarees made very poor targets for the bombers and about the only result of the bombing were to ruin their own installations and kill many of their own men.

When night fell, nearly all firing ceased and the Marines, knowing their objective had been reached attempted to withdraw, but couldn't combat the furious force of breakers hitting the reefs. They were split up in several small groups, each group believing they were the only ones left on the Island and with renewed desperation, they attempted to get past the breakers to the submarine, only a few got through while some were drowned and two were attacked by sharks. The rest, losing their weapons in the surf, went back to the beach and making sure each man had a hand grenade, one for some Japs and one for himself, they prepared to fight to the last man.

Dawn broke cool and clear on the little Island and with a better peace of mind they reconnoitered and sent scout to the other ends of the island and soon each group realized that most of the Raiders were still on the Island, including Col. Carlson and Major Roosevelt.

Setting in to finish wiping out the Japs. The Marines were in good spirits and grinned with satisfaction when a sniper would fall from the tops of trees.

Soon the Jap bombers returned and continued bombing their own troops and supplies.

The Raiders hugged the earth and raked the enemy with a scathing fire while the natives on the Island knowing the position of the snipers directed their fire. One of the native men, after a great deal of motioning and explaining, managed to let the Marines know he wanted a rifle, they readily gave it to him, whereupon he crept through the brush and accounted for eight of the yellow Japs.

The remainder of the Japanese becoming desperate, attempted a charge which failed miserably. Approximately seventeen Japs started the charge. None of them reached the Marines or inflicted any damage. They were rapidly cut down with automatic fire. Colonel Carlson and Major Roosevelt showed extreme courage dashing here and there, seemingly everywhere at once. Roosevelt stalked up and down the beach with raised pistol and spotting a Jap, he would take careful aim and kill the Nipponese, then coming back to raised pistol he would give the battle-cry of the Raiders — "Gung Ho!"

Many times, he repeated this performance accounting for a large number of the Japs.

"My Thoughts About Going to Guadalcanal"

By Don Gardner

I wanted to go to Guadalcanal! Guadalcanal --- a few months prior, very few people had heard of Guadalcanal, a mere Speck, an insignificant pin head in the South Pacific, one of thousands of volcanic formations that are scattered all over the vast Pacific Ocean.

Yes, a few months ago, no one was interested in Guadalcanal, another Japanese Base, but nothing made it especially significant to us.

But now it was different. The entire world knew about Guadalcanal, and the magnificent battle fought there by the U.S. Marines against overwhelming odds. Odds not only in men, but in planes and ships as well.

Yes, I certainly wanted to go to Guadalcanal. Here it was, the middle of October of 1942. The original landing there had taken place on August 7th of that same year.

I couldn't see ahead to count the many islands like Guadalcanal that lay ahead from there to Tokyo. Only this one Island seemed important, our first decisive offensive action against the enemy in World War II.

Guadalcanal was still capturing the headlines of the newspapers and consequently the interest and attraction of the American people.

It seemed as though if I couldn't be in this battle before it was over, it would be like actually losing a vital part of my anatomy. But the months were slipping by and although we were at an advanced base less than 500 miles from this historic battleground, we still hadn't made a move to join in the fight there.

The days went by and very little action was reported at Guadalcanal, we were sure the fighting was about over and we had missed it all, but even as our spirits reached a new low, we were called out for a battalion formation and informed by our Commanding officer, Lt. Col. Carlson, that we would be leaving for Guadalcanal in a very few days and that we definitely were not going for a picnic.

The next few days were spent in preparation for our embarkment to Guadalcanal, but as the hour approached, we heard that the Japanese had landed a sizable force at the very spot where we were supposed to land. Temporarily, at least, our part in the operation was postponed.

47

The postponement was very temporary however, and we again prepared to board ship. This time with skepticism and doubt. But the pre-named day found us aboard our ship before dark of that day

The ship was an old type Destroyer and we were familiar with the ship and the crew, as we had lived aboard her for two weeks at the Battle of Midway in June.

We pulled out of the harbor at the sunset followed by another Destroyer loaded with the rest of our men.

By the following morning we were well on our way to Guadalcanal. The wind was unusually high and piled up huge waves for us to wallow through; the aft part of the ship was flooded with waves of water making it a very uncomfortable and insecure place to stay so the fore part was well crowded while the wind and water had the rest of the ship practically to themselves.

The following Destroyer stayed behind us and well to one side of our wake.

I learned later that on a former trip, she had been following directly in the wake of the leading Destroyer and a depth charge had accidently came loose from the first ship and narrowly missed blowing the following ship to Kingdom Come!

"Guadalcanal Diary"

The following article was published in January 1981 in the "Soldier of Fortune Magazine". It is printed here with the permission of Lt. Col. Robert K. Brown, USAR (Ret.) Editor, Publisher, Soldier of Magazine NRA BOD.

Thank-you Sir.

BEHIND THE LINES IN
CAMBODIA

SOLDIER OF FORTUNE

The Jour... ...venturers

JANUARY
1981 $2.50

RAIDER DIARY
SWAPO STRIKES OUT
EQUAL OPPORTUNITY AIRBORNE

50

Story of a Marine Raider

THE
CREAM
OF THE
CORPS

By Arthur D. Gardner   Foreword by Jim Graves

51

Legend surrounded Carlson's Raiders as soon as traditionalist superiors reluctantly permitted Evans F. Carlson to form the Second Raider Battalion on 5 February 1942.

There was a dire need for heroes and legends then, as the United States staggered in defeat – its fleet destroyed and on the bottom of Pearl Harbor, its armies fleeing all over the Pacific from the seemingly invincible Japanese.

In Carlson, America found a man with the right combination of experience, political influence and determination to make a legend spring to life.

Carlson, a former Army officer who joined the Marine Corps in the 1930s, had considerable political pull through his friendship with Capt. Jimmy Roosevelt, the son of President Franklin D. Roosevelt. That enabled him to get his unit formed, despite considerable resistance from more conservative superiors within the Marine Corps.

When Japan invaded China in 1936, Carlson was sent there as an observer. He spent a considerable portion of his time in the Orient with the Chinese Communist 8th Route Army, and lessons he learned from it proved invaluable when the U.S. finally took the offensive against Japan.

In China, Carlson learned that a key to the Japanese army's success was its skill in flanking and infiltration tactics. But he also perceived that the flanking and infiltration teams were but lightly armed. Furthermore, by overemphasizing those tactics, they weakened their own flank and rear security -- making them vulnerable to attack.

Carlson felt that the way to beat the Japanese was to outflank and hit them from behind -- with superior firepower. His plan was to send small units of highly motivated, well-armed and tough men against the Japanese in commando-type operations.

His first requirement was the right kind of Marines. Carlson issued a call for volunteers and 3000 men signed up for interviews with him and his Executive Officer, Roosevelt.

Carlson told Roosevelt: "I won't take a man who doesn't give a damn about anything." Carlson stressed that point, because in China he learned that men intellectually committed to the war -- men who believed in it – made better soldiers than those who were either indifferent or suicidal.

Thus, the questions asked of prospective Raiders confused them. They ranged from: "What do you think of America? Why do you hate militarism? Do you think we ought to exterminate the Japs? Why do you want to join the Raiders? What's the war about? What're we fighting for?" to "Can you march 50 miles in a day? Can you cut a man's throat without hesitation?"

Arthur Gardner, author of the "Diary of a Marine Raider," says he was at first leery of volunteering for the unit, as scuttlebutt at San Diego held that only "Super Marines" need apply. "Well, I knew some of the men who were volunteering, and I knew they were no better than I was," said Gardner. "Most of them had been in the Marines a little longer (Gardner had just finished recruit training), but I knew they couldn't be that much better, and I wasn't about to admit they were until it was proven."

The legend still passed around today over Marine campfires is that the original Raiders were all big, mean and freed from the brig to form the unit. The truth is that a few did come from the brig, but most came straight from the graduating recruit classes in February 1942 -- young men from farms, cities and small towns of America.

Of the 3000 volunteers, Carlson found 2000 acceptable. But the Table of Organization (TO) permitted him to keep fewer than 1000. That problem was solved by intense training with special emphasis on hand-to-hand combat, jungle warfare and hit-and-run raid tactics like those used by British Commandos.

"Sometime toward the last of April 1942, Maj. Carlson gave us a bruising test to weed out the undedicated and the glory-seekers" explains Gardner. "After training unusually hard one day, we returned to our cook fires and pup tents at dark. After cooking rice in our canteen cups and browning some bacon . . . we prepared to get some sleep as we were all on the point of exhaustion.

"But the word passed to fall out with full combat gear, and we started a forced march that lasted until sunrise the next morning. Raiders straggled in all day since many had fallen by the road in utter exhaustion."

"Next morning Maj. Carlson told us that anyone who wanted to get out of the outfit was free to do so, and at least 200 took advantage of the offer."

That solved one of the TO problems. Another was solved because Carlson was a determined type, not likely to quit when told "No" by higher authority.

At that time, a Marine squad consisted of 10 men: a squad leader and nine riflemen, eight armed with M1 semiautomatic rifles and one with a Browning Automatic Rifle (BAR).

Carlson and his staff decided that rather than the large, difficult to maneuver 10-man squads, they wanted smaller units armed with more automatic weapons.

Carlson's concept was to break the squad up into fire groups, or fire teams, of three men – one to carry a BAR, one a Thompson .45 caliber submachine gun with a fifty-round drum magazine and one an M1. Since the fire groups could operate independently of each other, Carlson proposed that the fire-group leaders should receive promotions in proportion to their increased responsibilities.

When Carlson's organizational proposal worked its way up to higher headquarters, the traditionalists balked again. Carlson, being a dogged sort, rewrote his proposal once more. The second time around, approval came down for him to organize his troops in any manner he wished within his battalion strength limit. He also received permission to issue the automatic weapons, provided supply could produce them. (Carlson's basic concept of fire groups was later adopted by the entire Marine Corps.) It evolved into a four-man team – fire-team leader, a corporal; rifleman, BARman and assistant BARman, privates or PFCs. All but the BARman carried M1s.

Another Carlson innovation carried on today is the use of the Chinese expression "Gung Ho."

At some of the first training sessions in California, Carlson stunned his men -- enlisted and officers -- by telling them that the traditional rules under which Marines operated would not apply in the Raiders. Officers were to give up many of the privileges they were accustomed to and there would be periodic meetings where the men would sit and discuss training, America, democracy, militarism and other non-combat-related subjects.

Carlson called these sessions "ethical indoctrination." The purpose was to unify the men in pursuit of a common goal, understood by all.

"The Chinese have two words that mean 'working together,'" Carlson said. " 'Gung' meaning work and 'Ho,' meaning harmony. Gung Ho! Work Together!"

Carlson's Raiders trained in Hawaii until August 1942, when they were sent on a diversionary raid deep into the Central Pacific at Makin Island to draw off Japanese reinforcements against the 1st Marine Division landing at Guadalcanal and Tulagi.

Makin, some 2000 miles from Pearl Harbor, is in the Gilberts. Plans called for 221 Raiders to travel by submarine and launch the attack from rubber boats. The raid produced mixed results -- the Raiders killed 83 Japanese and lost 30 men from their own ranks. The Marines considered Makin less than a success due to problems with the rubber boats and the motors that came with them. Some men could not get through the heavy surf and back to the subs. Nine men left behind were beheaded by the Japanese on 16 October. However, that news was kept from the American public and Makin, which was the first victory on land scored by the Americans during World War II and captured public imagination.

Gardner did not make the Makin Island raid, but when the Raiders went to Guadalcanal, and later Bougainville, and cemented their legend, he was in the thick of it.

On Guadalcanal, the Raiders, aided and assisted by the ferocious, cannibalistic Solomon Islanders, pulled off one of the more incredible exploits of the war. In one month, they moved 150 miles behind Japanese lines, fought the enemy daily, killed more than 700 at the loss of only 17 Raiders killed and 17 wounded, and destroyed a Japanese artillery piece named "Pistol Pete" which had made life hell on Henderson Field for the 1st Marine Division.

Gardner served with the unit from start to finish and his terse, accurate and moving diary helps explain why the Raiders became a legend in their own time -- and remain so today.

For whenever Marines gather in their slopchutes, over canteen cups of coffee in the boondocks or barracks-room bull sessions, survivors of the Pusan Perimeter, Inchon Landing, Chosen Reservoir, Khe Sanh, the Rock Pile and the Arizona Territory will elaborate and enlarge their own exploits -- yet, inevitably, someone will say "but how about them Raiders? They were really tough."

Guadalcanal Diary

Nov. 8: Arrived at Guadalcanal about daybreak and were unloaded before noon. Some of us are on outposts along the river. There are crocodiles in this river.

Nov. 9: Loaded us in tank lighters and moved several miles up the coast. Set up a command-post bivouac. We have about 50 native guides with us to carry supplies and extra ammunition.

Nov. 10: Started out about 0700 and advanced about 10 miles. Rugged going. We had to ford three rivers; the Bevande, Tine and Balesuma. Set up a new bivouac here. We now have about 200 natives with us.

Nov. 12: Moved forward at daylight. The Japs had moved out during the night. We lost five men yesterday and buried them where they fell.

Nov. 13: We followed the Japs to the next river, the Asa Mona, and attacked them on both flanks. They are dug in so we dropped back and called for the 7th Marines' artillery to soften them up.

Nov. 14: Lost five more men yesterday. We escorted about 100 natives to the beach for more needed supplies -- especially ammunition.

Nov. 15: Rested all day. Dug wild potatoes, gathered red peppers, killed two tree lizards and made a stew. The lizards are green, about a foot long, and the meat is something like white meat from a chicken, if you have a good imagination. Had a Gung-Ho meeting. We are going into the interior to harass the Japanese in every way we can. We will take no prisoners under any circumstances. Any Raider caught stealing from another Raider will be executed without exception.

Nov. 16: Moved our base about three miles. Ran into occasional scattered Japs separated from their companies. Killed several of them. Lots of dead Japs lying around. We are bivouacked in a native village.

Nov. 17: On combat patrol. Lots of dead Japs; some knocked out by artillery. I found one alive but wounded and I shot him. He watched me with his eyes all the while. We ran into a bunch of cattle and shot eight of them. We had to send a runner back to the command post for natives to pack it in.

Nov. 18: We escorted a group of natives to the beach where the 7th Marines are based and brought back rice, tea, hardtack and ammunition.

Nov. 19: Carlson told our doctors to survey everyone not in A-1 condition. About 70 weeded out today.

Nov. 20: Guarding the supplies here now. We have outposts in trees all day and listening posts all night. Mosquitoes are terrible here. Impossible to sleep.

Nov. 21: Company headquarters joined us and set up there TBX *(Semi-Portable Radio Equipment of Low Power)* so now we have communication. They sent about 50 natives to pack supplies so we can move out but that isn't enough for what we have to pack, so we are waiting for further word.

Nov. 22: More natives showed up and we moved about four miles to the next river, the Toni. Set up bivouac.

Nov. 23: Moved about nine miles and made a new bivouac. Very rugged here with thick brush, vines, thorn stringers that we call "wait a minute vines" and a thick overhead that prevents the sun from ever getting to the floor. There is a small creek nearby.

Nov. 24: Had a combat patrol about six miles up the river. We were on the alert for Japs but didn't contact any. However, found lots of fresh sign and also one well-used trail that they have been using.

Nov. 25: On alert but rested some. About 40 men surveyed out and sent back to the beach.

Nov. 26: The doctors spend all day examining Marines to determine how good a shape they are in. Only the best can stay. Fifty or 60 were sent back today. One of our jobs in the interior will be to locate a 75mm gun the Japs have there and put it out of action. They have been shelling Henderson Field with it.

Nov. 27: Moved up the river straight inland for about nine miles. Sent out native scouts and there are several thousand Japanese close by. Can't build fires so we don't eat tonight.

Nov. 28: Went on combat patrol up an ungodly steep hill and located the East-West Trail on top of the ridge. Found where they had the 75mm set up but they had moved it. Ran into several Japs who were startled to see us. I killed two and believe we killed about a dozen altogether.

"We have Japs on all sides now"

Nov. 29: We are down to about 136 men and honed to what you might call a razor's edge. We moved about two miles further upstream. We have Japs on all sides of us now and are moving with utmost caution.

Nov. 30: We crossed a ridge so steep we used ropes to get over the top. Found the 75mm we were looking for and also two 37mm guns and destroyed all three. We crossed the East-West Trail, dropped into the upper Lunga River and ran into several hundred Japs. It started to rain and came down in bucketfuls. We killed 40 or 50 Japs and the rest escaped across the river. Finally quit raining about dark and we are bivouacked on a small stream. We decided to build fires and take our chances.

Dec. 1: Discovered this morning that we camped about 70 yards from a battalion of Japs all night. We surprised them at daylight and completely disorganized them. We killed at least 200 and the rest escaped across the river and into the jungle. Blackie was killed by a Jap sniper. We buried him here in this place. We made a cross for his head and covered it with tin from hardtack containers. Planes came over and dropped us bags of rice and some five-gallon tins of hardtack. They were so low the chutes didn't have time to open and we were out on our hands and knees picking up rice a grain at a time. The hardtack was not much more than crumbs.

Dec. 2: We formed a guard unit and accompanied our doctors while they made an inspection of Japanese medicines and supplies. Jap bodies are stinking really bad now. We buried two that were close to our sleeping area. Rain came down like a waterfall all afternoon.

Dec. 3: We moved about two miles down the river and split into two groups. Some continued on down the Lunga River toward the beach and the rest of us climbed a Japanese trail up a steep ridge. Near the top we ran into two Jap machine-gun nests and a number of Jap snipers and riflemen. Took us 1 ½ hours to wipe them out. By then it was dark. Someone came around asking for water for the wounded, but no one has any.

Dec. 4: Camped last night without grub, fires or water. Moved out this morning and over the first ridge contacted a large number of Japs dug in on a fringe of Jungle overlooking a grassy plain. They surprised us when they first opened fire, but we deployed and out maneuvered them and killed them all in about three hours. We lost three men last night and three more this morning besides wounded. Lt. Miller died today.

Dec. 5: We marched 27 miles' yesterday. We haven't eaten or had water for two days. We marched clear across Henderson Field. It is bigger than I had realized. Adams had a hand grenade in his back pocket and the and the pin worked out and exploded you know where. He was hurt pretty bad. The natives built another stretcher and packed him along with our other wounded. Goodbye, Guadalcanal.

Carlson Takes his Battalion AWOL

After the Guadalcanal operation we returned to our base at Espirito Santo where we were given the opportunity to rest and where we spent Christmas that year. Col. Carlson was determined that we should have some rest and relaxation and 3 February 1943 we boarded the U.S.S. *Henry T. Allen*, an old President Liner. We docked at Wellington, New Zealand, on 9 February, and after eight glorious days we reboarded another ship, the U.S.S. *Clymer*, and returned to Espirito Santo. This maneuver was frowned upon by Carlson's superior officers as he had taken us there without permission -- indeed, against orders. He was relieved of his command and returned to the States where he was described as a "Marine Corps Advisor." Later he was severely wounded on Saipan, but he survived his wounds.

****

Our new commanding officer was Col. Alan Shapley, a spit-and-polish Marine with a brilliant record and decorations for bravery during the Japanese attack on Pearl Harbor. We had lost our colonel, but his memory remained with us and we actually felt saddened and bereaved. By this time, the tempo of the war had changed, and the United States was now on the offensive in the South Pacific. No longer were hit-and-run raids of any purpose. Now it was hit-and-stay and our training was modified accordingly.

Our base was moved to Noumea, New Caledonia, and replacements began to swell our ranks until we were back to battalion strength. Training and maneuvers occupied most of our time night and day. Beachhead assaults were emphasized, and we spent weeks practicing them. By late October we were aboard ship bound for our next operation, which turned out to be Bougainville.

59

As on Guadalcanal, I kept a daily diary and the first entry is dated 1 November 1943.

"Bougainville Diary"

Nov. 1: Our destroyers opened up on Jap positions on Bougainville about 0500. About 0730 we hit the beach against moderate opposition. Our casualties were light, but Lt. Col. McCaffery, our executive officer, was killed as well as a few dozen others.

Nov. 2: Rained a lot last night. We dug fox holes and just waited for daylight. Our ships off shore shelled Jap positions all night. The Japs infiltrated our lines and threw hand grenades. Lots of rifle fire last night and all day today. We moved up and formed a front line. Jap planes were over twice today.

Nov. 3: We relieved the 3rd Raiders on the roadblock which the Japs have been hitting without letup. Our artillery opened up on the Japs about 0800. We received word that a large number of Japanese were in a native village and we took a combat patrol in there and killed most of them.

Nov. 4: Bad night. Some of the marines on the line got scared and threw hand grenades all night. There were no Japs where they were throwing the grenades. It rained all day and now the water is standing eight inches deep everywhere.

Nov. 5: They moved us back toward the beach in the evening and they fed us spuds and corned willie. Cats and tractors are bogged down in the mud everywhere you look. Mud is one foot to four feet deep everywhere.

Nov. 6: About 3,000 Marines came in this morning in LST's *(Landing Ship, Tank)*. Went on a combat patrol and we killed quite a few Japs. Lieutenant Hatt was walking along a trail with thick brush on either side when a Jap jumped out and cut his throat. We were so startled we didn't get a shot at him. Lieutenant Hatt died.

Nov. 7: Jap planes bombed us most of the night. Two Marines were killed near us. Japs landed three or four barges of fresh troops and they hit our roadblock today. They hit us hard but we held them back. Quite a few wounded-mostly face and legs. More rain and more rain.

Nov. 8: Jap planes bombed us all day. Heavy fighting on the line and it was all we could do to hold them back. Fought all day. Rainbow Campbell, Hijic and Ford were killed. I have no idea how many others.

Nov. 9: Third Raiders took over from us this morning. They had it hot and heavy gaining back what we had yesterday. We moved back up and dug in directly behind them in case they didn't hold the line. Our artillery pounds away 24 hours a day. It has to be tearing them up.

Nov. 10: We sat and lay in eight inches of water all night. Looked over Jap bodies all morning. Several hundred lying nearby. The 9th Marines took over the front lines and we moved back to rest. Our planes came in low and fast this morning and strafed the Japs about 200 yards in the front of us. Scared us as bad as it did the Japs.

Nov. 11: Jap planes dropped bombs all night. Lots of Marines cracking up and falling out with nerves. We figure we killed around 300 or 400 Japs up there. We've had a lot of casualties. Marko died today. He was hit in the back with a piece of Jap mortar shell.

Nov. 12: Resting up. We had a mail call of all things. I got 11 letters.

Raiders Support 21st Marines

Nov. 13: Japs hit the 21st Marines' lines so we moved to the front in the evening. We are dug in just behind the front lines in case they break through. Steady rifle and machine-gun fire. The stench from dead bodies is so bad here we can barely stand it.

Nov. 14: Our artillery started at 0900 and the fury of it was overwhelming. Our light tanks came up for support and then our planes bombed and strafed the Jap lines directly in front of us. The 21st Marines advanced the front lines about 200 yards against heavy opposition and we moved our lines up behind them. Hundreds of Japanese killed. We killed about 30 even back here. Dead Marines are lying all about. I understand our tanks accidentally killed some of the Marines when they ran over them. Vaught and I moved into a fox hole here that was already dug. We don't know if it was dug by Marines or Japs. There are six dead Marines lying about two feet from our foxhole. Been there since yesterday.

Nov. 15: The 21st Marines got scared last night and fired into the darkness until daylight. They even shot some of their own men. Details are bringing the dead Marines out. Many are fly blown beyond recognition and have no identification on them. The 3rd Raiders moved up and relieved us and we dropped back to rest. Dirty and crummy more than tired.

Nov. 17: Eight Jap planes came in low, without warning, about daylight and strafed us. Guaranteed to cure constipation. Then more planes right behind them and they kept it up for about an hour. There were 18 planes altogether. Lots of dead and wounded.

Nov. 19: We are on constant standby alert. Jap planes bombed most of the night. Killed seven near us and wounded five or six. You can hear the bombs whistling when they are coming down. They always sound like they are coming straight at you.

Nov. 20: Air raids all night. They dropped a lot of bombs about 0500 and set some gasoline stores on fire. Quite a few wounded coming down the trail today.

Nov. 21: Jap planes really bombed us last night and this morning. Bombers and some dive bombers. Got a few pretty close to us. We moved out about 1200 and dug in directly behind front lines. Japs are dropping 90mm mortars in here. We went on combat patrol beyond our lines and found two dead marines.

Nov. 22: We moved up and took over the front lines. Japs lobbed 90mm mortars in here all night. Killed seven and wounded a bunch. Japs had foxholes dug here and we are moving into them. Constant small arms fire now. We are in the hills now and the Japs are dug in about 200 yards away. We can hear them talking and shouting orders. There was a dog fight overhead today. We saw three planes shot down.

Nov. 23: Artillery and mortar fire 24 hours a day. We moved forward, pushed the Japs back and set up a new line of defense. We gained about 400 yards. We have G Company on our right flank. A U.S destroyer lying offshore is firing over our heads into Jap positions. Jap mortar fire has slacked off some. I think they are afraid to use it because they fear our return fire.

Nov. 24: Our artillery fired without letting up all night. Two Jap mortar shells landed almost on top of us this morning. Knocked out a bunch of our men. Buddy Barritt was killed and four were wounded. Jefferson and several others were badly shell-shocked. We got eight turkeys already cooked up here on the front lines. Supposed to be for Thanksgiving. Lots of rifle fire today on both sides.

Nov. 25: We laid down a 10-minute artillery barrage this morning and as soon as it was over we advanced about 300 yards before we met opposition. We ran into about a platoon of Japs dug in on a knoll. They lobbed a lot of knee mortar rounds and threw hand grenades down on us. Lawson, Peterson and I made two trips to the 9th Marines' command post under heavy fire. How they kept from hitting us I can't possibly understand. The bullets whistled by like mosquitoes. It was afternoon before we could outflank them, and we killed them all. There were about 60.

Nov. 26: We moved out this morning and tied in with the 9th Marines. Then we advanced about 900 yards. We were supposed to tie in with F Company on the left, but they weren't there, so we dropped back 300 yards and we still couldn't find them. We are set up here sticking out like a sore thumb. We found some big Jap bivouacs today. They were all over this area. Lots of artillery hits in here and I suppose that ran them out. Lots of Japs buried shallow and the stench is unbelievable. There are about 30 unburied.

Nov. 27: Contacted F Company this morning. Another combat patrol and we found another big Jap bivouac area just ahead of where we were yesterday. We estimated at least 1,200 dead Japs knocked out by our artillery. Smith and I went across the draw and found numerous dead Japs and a well-used trail with communication lines strung along it. We were relieved by the 9th Marines and dropped back.

Off the Line

Nov. 28: We got two hot meals today - the first for some time and it made the sweat pour off us. We are on a moment's notice to move out if we are needed. Took a good bath in a stream nearby and felt good to be cleaned up. We talk to the 53rd SeaBees near here and they think we are great. They named one of their roads "Marine Drive" for us.

Dec. 7: We marched five miles to front lines packing grub and ammunition to the paratroopers.

Dec. 14: The Japs hit the 9th Marines hard today and our artillery really tore them up.

Dec. 21: I was admitted to Hospital C Medical with malaria.

Dec. 25: We had spam and sliced pineapple for Christmas dinner.

Dec. 26: Checked out of hospital and reported back to my company on front lines. They have trenches dug three and four feet deep and are just sitting tight.

Dec. 27: Japs lobbed a lot of mortars in on us last night. Chick Madsen and two other Marines were killed.

Dec. 29: We went on combat patrol about 2,000 yards forward of our lines and didn't see any live Japs.

Jan. 11: Army troops relieved us and we dropped back to the beach. We will go aboard ship tomorrow. This island is what I would call "secured".

The Raiders were doomed. We were to be disbanded and reformed as the 4th Marine Regiment, the only regiment that refused to surrender its colors in the Philippines. (The 4th Marine Regiment survivors burned their colors and headed for the bush when ordered to surrender.)

It was a sad day for us but it was inevitable. One Raider wrote a poem that started, "They are doing away with the best they've got and throwing us in with the common lot." While it was a nice thought, it was not necessarily true. Put any Marine into combat and he is likely to be just as effective, just as good, as any other Marine.

On Guadalcanal the separation took place. Those of us who had left the States on 9 May 1942 were referred to as "The Old Raiders," and we were put aboard ships bound for the United States. The others went to the 4th Marine Regiment. Of the 900 who had started out there were now exactly 231.
Gung Ho.

ABOUT THE AUTHOR

Arthur D. Gardner enlisted in the U.S. Marines shortly after the onset of World War II. He was accepted as a member of Carlson's Second Marine Raider Battalion and sent for intensive training near San Diego, Calif. On 9 May 1942 the Raiders shipped out for further training at Oahu, Hawaii. At the end of that month they were sent to Midway and in November to Guadalcanal.

Gardner declares, "I carried a Browning Automatic Rifle (BAR) the entire time I was in the Raiders. It was a beautiful weapon and I would not have traded it for any other available at that time. It weighed 18 pounds and each 20-round clip weighed one pound. I always tried to keep my ammo supply at 30 clips, which I carried in bandoleers slung across my shoulders."

After action with the Raiders, Cpl. Gardner returned to the States on leave. He went back overseas in September 1944 and saw action in the Okinawa campaign the following spring. At the end of the war, he was sent to Tientsin, China, where he spent the remainder of his enlistment. He returned to the U.S. in February 1946.

—M.L. Jones

Lt. Col. Evans F. Carlson (center) washes his feet and changes socks while two Raiders stand guard on upper Lunga River. Photo: Arthur D. Gardner

Above: Bearded, muddy Marine Raiders trudge down trail from front after three weeks of fighting on Bougainville.

Sgt. Maj. Vuzu holds head of Japanese soldier killed at Guadalcanal. Natives frequently decapitated Japanese soldiers after Raiders killed them. Vuzu, a member of police prior to Japanese invasion, was made honorary Sgt. Maj. by the USMC for his assistance in the Guadalcanal campaign. He warned Marines of impending Japanese counterattack and was instrumental in getting other islanders to serve as scouts, guides and bearers. In July 1979 Sgt. Maj. Vuzu became Sir Sgt. Maj. Vuzu when knighted by Queen Elizabeth for his wartime service to the allies. Photo: Arthur D. Gardner

This ends the 'Soldier of Fortune" article.

"Bougainville Raid"

A guy comes in and says, "They're loading our ship now and we're going aboard in three or four days." We laugh, "Who told you that?" We ask him. We've been hearing the same thing with little variation for the past two weeks, so of course we were dubious. "You'll see," the news bearer retorts, as he starts squaring his gear away as though he were actually going aboard in the next five minutes.

Naturally, we were surprised when the Sergeant calls us out within a half hour and tells us to get our sea bags packed and all web gear camouflaged with green paint, so's to be ready to board ship whenever they tell us to.

We aren't excited like we were the first time we were going into action, mostly we're just mad, because of all the work we see ahead of us within the next few days. We know we'll be up all day and most of the night, until the ship is loaded, and we are all aboard in our compartments.

All the "new men", who were replacements for our guys killed last time, are running around like a chicken with its head cut off and accomplishing just about as much. "How many blankets are you taking in your combat pack?" They ask us. "None," we tell 'em, "Don't you know it rains every night in the jungle and your blanket will soak up water like a sponge? Just take your poncho and shelter half, easier to carry."

They keep asking us about this and about that, until we aren't even sure ourselves what we're supposed to be doing. We finally get our sea bags packed and cinched up. Then we sat down to smoke a cigarette. The Sergeant comes in and says, "They changed the order on what to carry in your pack, you've got to take your mosquito net and an extra pair of shoes."

This makes us feel very unhappy, because either the shoes or the net will be in the bottom of the sea bag. After a short period of fruitless cursing and moaning, we unpack the sea bags and get the required gear, afterwards repacking and recinching.

After the orders have been changed on what to carry in your pack a few more times, so we finally get squared away and start wondering where we are going to go this time.

"Maybe we're going to Tokyo", quips one of the new guys. "You'll probably settle for Tokyo before this job is over," we tell him.

68

"I had a heart to heart talk with the 'Old Man,' he says we're making a beach head in San Francisco," some wise guy pops off.

We ignore this character and go on with our letters to mom, pop, and the girlfriend.

We're glad when they finally tell us that we're going aboard the ship tomorrow. I went to the movie this night, because we probably won't see another one for a long time. It's a good picture and I enjoyed it, forgetting temporarily about going into action in a few days.

Reveille's an hour earlier than usual the next morning, we get up and break our G.I. cots down so they can be stacked in an empty tent, we wash up and make a run to the mess hall and grab some chow and coffee. Everybody's in a rush, the Sergeant is roaring to get a move on while the Lieutenant is egging him on.

"All right, come alive, let's get out here and fall in," the Sergeant bellows. We fall out in the Company street with packs and weapons; they call the roll and report three men missing; one at the head, one still eating, he's probably one of those guys that really believes in stocking up in case rations get low, and the other one's whereabouts is unknown.

After a little uncomplimentary shouting on the Sergeant's part, everyone is present and ready to shove off.

The Lieutenant comes over, "Take off your packs and stand at ease men," he tells us, "We may not leave for an hour or two." We sat down and smoke cigarettes and adjust our pack straps; we talk about the things that happened last time we were in battle. The new guys listen and ask us questions.

"Just use your head for something besides a Jap target and you'll make out alright," we tell them. The Lieutenant comes back, "get your packs on and stand by," he says, the trucks come up and we load on them fighting for a seat on the side, so we won't have to stand in the middle. We're cramped and uncomfortable during the ride to the docks, but we whistle at the native girls and they smile and wave at us.

We pile off the trucks and drop our packs again while we wait for the boats to take us out to the ship which is anchored in the bay. A boat pulls up in a few minutes and we get our packs on again and walk down there, we have to take the packs off though and load the boat with chow and ammunition. It's late afternoon before we get out to the ship and climb aboard. We're hungry and start looking for the galley, all they've got is sandwiches because they are loading rations in the hold under the mess hall, so we get a corned beef sandwich and go top-side to watch while they finish loading the ship.

Its crowded along the rail and on the deck, Marines are sprawled under the life boats and even in the trucks that are lashed on the open deck.

They finish loading the ship and all the boats are hoisted aboard and secured, and we listen for the rattle of the anchor chain which will mean we are getting under way, but when I finally get in the chow line they still haven't made a move as far as we can see. It's hot aboard the ship if you have to sleep in the hold at night, so as soon as chow is over, I get my canvas shelter half and pick out a sheltered spot topside to spend the night.

There's still some space on the tarpaulin covered hold, but no protection in case of rain, it doesn't look like it will rain anyway, so I spread my canvas there and stretch out with just my shoes off and look at the super structure while it gets dark and the stars start coming out.

It's just breaking dawn when I wake up, there is a lot of noise and shouting, I get up and look around, the sailors are running past with their life jackets and steel helmets, I look toward shore but there is nothing but water on all sides, we were at sea somewhere. I notice the sailors are manning their AA guns, it scares me for a minute, I wonder if the Japs are attacking, it is a sub or Zero's?

It turns out to be the routine General quarters held every morning, so I lay down again, but some sailors come by in a minute washing down the deck, so I grab my shoes and canvas and get out of the way of the splashing salt water. The Marines are lining up for chow already so I get in line and gaze out over the ocean until the line swings below deck where there is nothing to do but wait until the line finally leads you into the mess hall.

The guy in front of me gets sick from the motion of the ship rocking and throws up in the passageway. It makes me feel a little sick myself to see him, but I steel myself against it, after I eat, I felt better. We play hearts on deck all morning, then go to chow again. It's dull with nothing to do and we'll be glad when we get where we're going, so we can get off the ship and have more room to move around.

After evening chow, we play cards until dark and have trouble finding a place on deck to sleep. I find a spot between the rail and a ventilator and go to sleep there. It rains off and on all night, and I get pretty wet. It's so hot below deck that I decide to weather it out and get dry when the sun comes out the next morning.

The next day we join a convoy with Destroyer escorts. It's a big convoy and we whistle to ourselves; it's going to be a large-scale operation. After a couple more days, we're getting pretty close and we've been in enemy water all day. That night the Jap's spot us and their planes come over and drop flares. We can hear the motors but it's hard to see the planes. The flares light up the water all around and we can see the other ships in the convoy as well as if it were broad daylight, they drop a few bombs pretty close but not close enough to do any damage, the transports don't fire back, the Japs are probably wishing we would so they could get a better idea of where we are at.

The sound of their motors finally dies out, and its dark and silent again except for the shuddering of the ship's beams, as she bucks the waves.

We aren't allowed to sleep top side this last night, so I go down to the galley and lay on the floor for a while, it's too hot to rest so I get a cup and drink coffee and smoke cigarettes until they start serving breakfast.

I go through the line and get a sandwich and a hardboiled egg. I decided I wasn't very hungry, so I ate the egg and threw away the sandwich.

The ship speaker buzzes, and they announce for all troops to report to their compartments. It's just starting to get light in the east, we know it won't be too long now until we hit the beach.

We get our packs squared away and run an oil rag through the rifle bore again. It's hot in the compartment and the air is heavy and stifling. I try my pack on to make sure the straps are adjusted right. It feels alright, so I put it on the deck by my rifle and get my steel helmet and cartridge belt. The pockets are full, and I've got two extra bandoleers, I wonder how much ammunition I'll use, or if I'll have a chance to use any or not.

Everything is in order, so I set down. Then I look around at the guys I'm going in action with. They are good men and I feel confident and elated about meeting the enemy with these fellows I know so well. The sweat is running off my nose in a tiny stream and my eyes are smarting from it. I wish we would

71

get the order to disembark but the ship is still moving, and I know it will be a little while yet. Someone passes a jar of green grease paint for camouflaging your face. I put some on, there is too much sweat and it comes right off.

The speaker buzzes and we reach for our gear, but they are just telling us to stand by, so I light another cigarette and inhale the smoke in long deep puffs.

We can feel the ship slowing down and the rolling has stopped so we know we are in a bay or a sheltered spot close to land. We can hear explosions now and it makes me uneasy. We wish we were topside so we could see what's going on. The ship vibrates and we hear the hollow boom of our guns going off. We wonder what they are shooting at and if there are any Jap planes up there, the explosions can be heard in a continuous barrage now and we are getting impatient to get out of the hold.

I think what it would be like if our ship was hit and we went down without ever getting to the top again. It's four decks up to open air and I know we'd never get out.

I wonder if my folks would find out how I was killed. The notice would say 'killed in action'. It probably wouldn't mention that I died like a rat in a trap.

The ship vibrates from the recoil of the five-inch gun on the fan tail, we look at each other and grin, "Boy, they're giving them Japs hell".

The speaker buzzes and we look toward it, "Standby to disembark in 5 minutes," it announces.

I grab my gear and slip into it. I look at my knife and it's pretty dull. I should have sharpened it, but it's too late now, we're going over the side in 5 minutes.

My rifle is new and the oil glistens in the Smoky light. I looked through the barrel and it looks good, I pet the stock affectionately. It's a good weapon and I like it.

I draw my sleeve across my forehead and the rest of the camouflage paint comes off with the sweat. The pack is getting heavy now, so I lean against the bulkhead to rest.

I can still hear the guns firing, it makes one impatient. I wonder why they have to keep firing so long.

It's been more than 5 minutes now, but we can't go up until they pass the word on the speaker, so I cuss and wonder why they don't let us go up. We want some fresh air.

We aren't supposed to load our rifles until nearly to the beach. It worries me because I'm afraid I might forget to load it at all. I pull the bolt to the rear and leave it there so I can't help but notice it and load the rifle at the right time.

The speaker buzzes and we know this is it. They give us the word and we go up the ladders on the double. It seems like miles to the top and I keep looking up for the sign of daylight so, when I come out on the deck, I'm weak and nearly out of wind. Men are already swarming down the cargo nets.

I hook my rifle onto my pack so it won't catch in the net and start climbing down. I'm glad now of the practice we've had. It's easy going down the net. I turn loose and drop the last few feet and grab the net to steady it for the men still coming down. It doesn't take long for the boat to get full and pull away to make room for the next boat. Marines are already starting down the net again before the boat is secured beneath.

The Lieutenant tells us to get down in the boat, but no one gets down so he doesn't say anything because he wants to watch as much as we do. We're going in a circle now waiting for the other boats before we start in to shore.

I see the shore about a half a mile away and i gaze at it to see if I can locate any movements or sign of Japs. There's a smoky haze hanging over the land from exploding shells and bombs, the trees are torn and frayed. I figure a lot of those Japs are already out of business and we should be able to get in without too much opposition.

The Destroyers are setting around in a semicircle still pouring a heavy barrage into the Jap installations on the beach. They look good when the guns go off and you can see them belch fire and gray smoke.

While I'm watching, one of the destroyers quits firing and takes off at a pretty good clip. I hear a plane roaring glanced up to see a dive bomber coming in on the circle of destroyers. The AA guns open up, but he keeps diving right into them, he drops his bomb and I feel fascinated as I follow it with my eyes until it hits the water, a scant twenty-five yards from the ship. The Jap pulled out of the dive to pass directly over the ship he meant for a victim, but it looks like he will get away. I cuss under my breath, but as he starts to climb for altitude, a thread of black smoke starts pouring out behind the plane and gets denser until he is nearly hidden from view, when the gas finally bursts into flames the plane explodes and I watch the pieces fall toward the ocean. I wonder which piece is the pilot.

Another streak of smoke catches my eye and I look up just in time to see a parachute open and a second later the plane was a massive flame.

That was a zero and I wonder what the pilot is thinking about, as I watch him coming down in the chute.

There are a lot of planes overhead now and it's hard to tell which are ours and which are the Japs. I see two more crash down, but the pilots don't get out. Usually they explode too quick.

I look toward shore again and see that we're heading in, zig-zagging to make a poorer target. We get pretty close and the destroyers are still firing. I get a little worried now and wonder if they will stop before we hit the beach.

The Lieutenant tells us to get down and this time we do. I look at my rifle and notice the bolt is open, so I load a clip and snap the safety.

There isn't enough room in the boat and my legs are cramped from squatting and being crowded. But I don't want to sit down because it wouldn't be able to get up and out of the boat fast enough when they let the ramp down.

I feel scared now and I wonder if there will be very many Japs on the beach. I think about an advertisement I saw in a magazine showing men going into the beach in a boat like this one. The ad said, "What will you be doing 10 minutes from now?"

"Standby," the Navy coxswain shouts above the noise of the motor, we brace ourselves and the boat grates on the sand and throws us forward. He guns the motor and the boat goes up another couple of feet on the beach.

I can hear bullets hitting the sides of the boat and I know what they are. "If I can get across the beach and into the jungle, I'll be on even terms with them, "I think to myself.

The cable screeches as they lower the ramp and I raise up ready to run out, I run up on the ramp and jump off before it's clear down. I can hear quite a few ricochets and I tried to brace my flesh in case I get hit.

I wonder if I'm already hit and can't feel it, sometimes it numbs you and you can't tell until later.

I see a man fall in front of me, a second later, another one goes down a little to the side.

I know men are landing on the beach on both sides of us, but I don't look because I'm concentrating on getting into the jungle. I'm not scared now, just excited. I wish I could see something to shoot at.

We hit the deck as soon as we reach the jungle underbrush. I lay there gasping for breath and wonder to myself how I got across the beach without getting hit. Some of the guys are firing back at the Japs now, but there's too much brush in front of me and I can't see. I crawl forward a little way and the ground slopes away to a narrow slough in front of us. I can see men in single file on the other bank and I wonder how any marines got over there so quick. Then I know they aren't Marines, their Japs trying to get away. I looked through my sights at the one in the rear and I feel good when he drops as I squeeze the trigger.

More of the Marines are out where they can see the Japs now and as more of the Japs become casualties, they become panicky. Some stop and fire back at us but most of them run out of sight.

We keep firing at the few remaining on the opposite bank, until there is no return fire. A squad is sent over to make sure they are knocked out. The slough is about waist-deep; We stand by ready to give protective fire, if necessary, while the Marines wade across.

Some of the Japs are wounded and there is a few more shots while they finish them off. We move up the beach about 100 yards. There we are given instructions to dig foxholes and keep a sharp lookout for the enemy.

There's quite a bit of firing on both flanks, but our part of the line is pretty quiet.

I don't feel like digging a temporary Foxhole, so I kneel on the ground in the jungle.

Is there any sign of Life over there now after a few minutes, I get tired of watching there so I go out a few yards toward the back where I can see what's going on over the bay.

There is quite a bit of firing on both flanks, but our part of the line is pretty quiet.

I didn't feel like digging a temporary foxhole, so I kneel on the ground and watch toward the jungle.

There isn't any sign of life over there now and after a few minutes, I get tired of watching there so I go out a few yards toward the beach where I can see what's going on over the bay.

There are still a lot of Jap planes up there and I watch them for a while and see several
more shot down.

Some of the guys are getting their foxholes pretty deep now, but I'm still not inclined to dig one of my own.

I hear the motor of a plane coming in pretty close and I wonder what it's doing at such a low altitude. A second later, I find out exactly what he's doing so low, because he opens fire with his machine guns and starts strafing the beach. We can hear the explosions as the bullets leave the guns and then we hear even better the sound of the bullets hitting the sand around us. I can't remember ever being this scared. It seems worse, because I know I can't do anything but lay here and hope none of the bullets hit me. My whole body seems to wrench and I wait for the bullets to enter my flesh. But the plunk into the sand a few feet away. After he pulls up and gone, I'm still okay.

I'm thoroughly in the mood by now to dig a foxhole and I figure if I could dig from now on, it would never get deep enough.

I get my shovel in gear and started scratching the dirt away. But before I hardly get started the plane comes over strafing us again. I try to get completely in the tiny hole I've got dug and succeed to a certain extent. This time he pulls up before the bullets reach us and I resume my digging. The plane comes over several more times and inflicts a number of casualties among the troops both on the beach and in the Higgins boats, yet in the water.

One of our men a few yards up the beach has both legs shot completely off. They apply tourniquets and take him back aboard ship.

I wonder if he will live and figure that he probably won't.

Just as I get my foxhole to a decent depth, they pass the word to move out so I reluctantly leave my little haven of refuge and fall in place as my squad moves out.

We go directly up the beach for a couple hundred yards and cut inland on a well used Jap trail. After a little way, we find ourselves in a clearing. There are several huts erected with mosquito nets strung up in them, where the Jap officers had probably slept. There are some clothes hanging on a makeshift clothesline to dry and their breakfast is still in cups and pots uneaten. Several dead Japs are laying in and around the clearing, so I figure they don't need their breakfast much anyhow. A marine that doesn't looked over 17 is sitting on a log a few feet from a couple of dead Japs. He's got a bandage on his nose and I found out later that a sniper slug took a little groove out of the bridge of his nose.

We go to the edge of the clearing and take our packs off. Then, with our weapons we start scouting out the trees and area for any possible live nips. There are shallow trenches dug all around the beach and every hundred or so a well-built pill box. We scout all the pill boxes. But we're too late. Because there are only dead Japs in them.

We move out again in a few minutes and go inland about 300 yards. The jungle is quiet now and only occasionally are shots heard. Apparently the Japs were on the run for the hills.

We dig foxholes again and eat one of our rations. The sun is getting pretty hot by now and my canteen is getting pretty dry, but the water situation is soon solved when one of the fellows strikes water in his Foxhole after digging a couple of feet.

The Lieutenant comes by and we ask him what the dope is. Apparently, everything is running pretty good.   Although we lost our Commanding Officer on the beach.

The Lieutenant tells us about the Chaplain, who voluntarily came in with the first wave, a Jap snipers bullet entered his helmet from the front, cut a gash in his head, went whistling on out the back of his helmet. However, it never fazed him. He is still keeping up, and is noticeably proud of his bandage.

We soon move out again and continue inland where we strike to the Piva Trail. After a little ways of bucking jungle.

The trail is wide and well beaten and we keep on it for several hundred yards until we come to the area where Battalion headquarters are setting up. We stop there a few minutes while our Captain is getting instructions.

The fellow that drives the hospital Jeep comes over and shoots the breeze with us. He's a good Joe, but I envy him a little because I know he probably won't have to be on the front line much, if any, and will get better chow then we will. The next day we found out the Jeep driver was killed that night by a Jap mortar shell that lit in the hospital bivouac area.

We moved out, up the trail again, and they pass the word back to watch the trees for snipers because they have been firing at Marines walking along the trail all day.

They don't bother to shoot at us though. We then turn off the trail and enter the jungle without mishap. It's late afternoon by now, and we start setting up our defenses for the night.

We have the main line of defense, but there is another outfit just ahead of us on the trail with the road block, so we are pretty sure the Japs will never get back where we are unless they put up a better battle than I think they are capable of.

The spot for my foxhole is right next to a pretty fair-sized tree and I have a hard time cutting through the roots in order to get it deep enough. I dig a hole about 6 feet long and 14 inches deep and let it go at that. It's already getting deep; if I dig any deeper, I'll have to lay in water all night. Right in front of me is a small slough and a lot of thick jungle. So I figure if any Japs come through there, they'll make a lot of noise and I'll be ready for them.

I get the second which is from 9:30 till 10:00. I've gotten my canteen full of water from a hole we dug at the edge of the slough and I eat another ration before I go to watch. By the time my watch is up its pitch dark and I had a hell of a time crawling over about 10 yards to wake the next guy up. I finally find my Foxhole again and crawl in with the mosquito net and try to get a little sleep. Our artillery is coming over all the time and landing out in front of us. The Japanese artillery is coming from the other way and most of it lands in front of us too.

Some of them sound pretty close and I begin to wish my Foxhole was deeper, water or no water.

I'm just getting used to the shells whistling over and exploding on ahead when I hear a different sounding explosion. It's closer and not so loud. I'm trying to figure out if it was a hand grenade or not, when several more of the same explosions sound off. I know darn well now that they are hand grenades, but I don't know if they are ours, or the Japs, or both.

It's in the neighborhood of the roadblock ahead of us and some of the shrapnel finds Its way back to where we are and clips the leaves as it goes by.

A few rifle shots can be heard up there now and I figure somebody is catching hell. I try to look out of my foxhole. But it's so dark, I can't even tell when my eyes are above the top of my foxhole. I'm glad now for the time I've spent in the jungle in action before. All the close sounds don't bother me, because I'm fairly certain they are just birds, and lizards and bugs. Some of our new men aren't so lucky though. They figure each one of those sounds is a Jap sneaking up on them. A few rifle shots are heard along our line now and it makes me leery. Because I don't know for sure whether they are shooting at Japs or only noises they figure are Japs.

I finally get used to all the racket and ease my mind with the thought that men are on watch all along the line. So, I get a little sleep in spite of the mosquitoes.

The man on watch at dawn comes along the line and makes sure everybody is awake. I'm cramped and stiff from sleeping in the hole so as soon as it gets broad daylight, I get out and stretch my muscles. Everybody has a different idea about digging a foxhole and I see Marines crawling out of all sorts of holes in the ground. Most of them are on the order of my own, where you can lay down with your rifle at your side. Some are dug straight down like a well with only standing or sitting room. Others are 4 or 5 ft deep as well and long enough to lay down in.

I get my gear ready to move out on a moment's notice, leaving out a ration for breakfast.

The rations are marked: breakfast, dinner, and supper, but usually we don't care what we eat when, it doesn't make much difference if we should eat a supper unit for breakfast. With men on watch we stand by for word to move out, but after a couple of hours, no word has been passed. So, I make a cup of hot coffee, using small heat tablets which don't make any smoke, yet throw out considerable heat. If you can get them lit. Getting them started is quite a chore in itself.

After 0900 the word is passed to get in our foxholes within a few minutes, as the pack howitzers, set up back of us, are going to start shelling the Japs at 0910.

I sit down near my foxhole and light a cigarette and wait for the barrage to start.

I wonder why the Japs didn't put up more of a fight then they did instead of running for the hills. I also wonder if I'll be alive tomorrow at this time, or even a minute from now.

I wonder if this is the worst fight we're going to have with the Japs, or if they will be back again in greater numbers. I'd always had the impression there were several thousand Jap troops on this island and I wonder where they are at. I hope they won't come but I know they will sooner or later, if they are here.

The barrage starts with a terrible fury, and I see how jumpy I am. I get in my Foxhole in case there are any short rounds and listen to the shells whistle over.

I can hear the report of the guns, followed a few seconds later by the sound of the shell overhead and then the explosions that follow as the shell lights out in front.

The shells sound a lot like leaves rustling and keep giving me the impression they are actually passing through the leaves directly overhead.

The barrage lasts about 20 minutes and when it's over we start moving out toward the trail again.

We don't know where we're going now but we suspicion it won't be a picnic at any rate.

As we're moving up the trail, we hear airplanes pretty low but don't think too much about it until they open up with machine guns and drop a few bombs. We hit the jungle on both sides of the trail, and I look up as they zoom overhead and see a red circle on the wings instead of that familiar star were used to.

They return again later in the day despite resistance of our own fighter planes.

There is quite a bit of firing ahead of us at times, with long stretches of silence in between.

We only move up the trail a couple of hundred yards and then we dig in again. It is clear and hot until late afternoon and then the very heavens seem to open up and pour water down on us in bucketful's. We are drenched and miserable. But merely the fact that the rain stops after about an hour, is enough to make us cheerful again.

By the time we get settled the day is nearly gone, we dig our foxholes for the night and heat a canteen cup of coffee to wash the "K" ration down.

The second night is nearly identical to the first except there are not as many hand grenades exploding, however there is considerably more rifle and machine-gun fire, both ours and the enemy's.

The next morning another terrific artillery barrage is laid down and immediately after it is over, we move out to the trail in a column and eventually the word gets around that we are going to relieve the 3rd Raiders on the roadblock. By this time, with two horrible nights behind us, the word "Roadblock" has assumed a very ominous sound. Even as we are sitting by the trail trying to relax. Stretcher bearers are coming by with their grisly loads on the stretchers, Marines with shrapnel and bullet wounds as well as knife and bayonet cases.

I personally suspicion that some, if not all, the knife wounds were inflicted by other Marines. Not sure who they were touching in the dark, but that doesn't make me feel any better about the whole business.

We finally get settled on the roadblock about noon and start making minor repairs on the fox holes that are already dug.

There is no action now or any sign of Japs, and all of us are hoping it will stay that way throughout the night.

Shortly after noon, we move out up the trail on a combat reconnaissance patrol. Our objective apparently is a native village about 500 yards ahead. The point is composed of one squad of riflemen supported by a 30-caliber machine gun section. As they come in sight of the village, they spot a number of Jap soldiers, apparently taken by surprise. The machine guns are quickly set up and a number of the little brown men are sent to join their ancestors before, the remainder get into the jungle to escape.

We don't follow the Nips past the village but merely send one platoon in to scout the huts. After a thorough search without finding any live Japs, we reverse the column and move back to the roadblock. The incessant rain starts pounding down again and we curse and try to shield our weapons from the downpour. By dusk, the rain has stopped, and we settle down for the night, not forgetting for a minute that we are the extreme point of the beachhead. The night later proved to be pretty much of a joke; though it wasn't the least bit funny at the time.

Silence prevailed until about an hour after dark when the jungle quiet was suddenly and rudely shattered by an explosion not ten yards to our front. My heart was in my throat and I hardly dared to breathe for the next few tense moments. Then I heard a sharp pop, such as a match head might make upon being struck, followed five seconds later by another explosion identical to the first. I heaved a sigh of relief as I was positive it was our own hand grenades. During the night around 30 grenades were thrown as well as a couple of our own concussion grenades. The shrapnel was flying overhead at a pretty good clip, but as long as everyone kept their head down, there was really very little danger as the grenades were all being thrown from our positions out to the front.

SECTION III

First Marine Division
Fleet Marine Force
c/o Postmaster, San Francisco, California

Division Circular
Number space 38A - 42

Citation of 2nd Raider Battalion
For Outstanding Service.

From the operational records of this division it appears that the 2nd Raider Battalion, while attached to this division, took the field against the enemy at Aola Bay on 5 November 1942. For a period 30 days this battalion, moving through difficult terrain, pursued, harried and by repeated attacks destroyed an enemy force of equal or greater size and drove the remnants from the area of operations. During this period the battalion, as a whole or by detachments, attacked the enemy wherever and whenever he should be found in a repeated series of carefully planned and well-executed surprise attacks. In the latter phase of these operations the battalion destroyed the remnant of enemy forces and bases on the upper Lunga river and secured valuable information of the terrain and the enemy line of operations. In these battles the enemy suffered 400 kills and the loss of his artillery, weapons, ammunition and supplies whereas the battalion losses were limited to 18 killed. For the consummate skill displayed in the conduct of operations, for the training, stamina and fortitude displayed by all members of the battalion and for its commendably aggressive spirit and high morale the commanding General cites to the 1st Marine Division the Commanding Officer, Officers and Men of the 2nd Raider Battalion.

/S/ A. A. Vandegrift
Major General., U. S. Marine Corps

While on combat patrol with Carlson's Second Marine Raider Battalion, we were ambushed by two Japanese machine guns and several snipers and rifleman. In my daily diary, I made the following entry: "Dec. 4 1942: Camped last night without grub, fires or water. Moved out this morning and over the first ridge contacted a large number of Japs on a fringe of jungle overlooking a grassy plain. They surprised us when they first opened fire, but we deployed and outmaneuvered them and killed them all in about three hours. We lost three men last night and three more this morning besides wounded. Lt. Miller died today." I wrote this poem for Lt. Miller:

Ambush!

Into the fetid jungle mud,
rank with death and stained with blood,
Marines move through the gloomy space
to seek those hiding in this place.

The noise comes bursting through the trees,
machine guns searching for our knees.
From mortal man to lump of clay…
Lt. Miller died today.

Marines now knowing what to do,
for facing death is nothing new.
Bitterness dwells with us there,
on the ground and through the air.

And over all the crashing sound
as mortars burst; machine guns pound.
What other lines could more portray?
Lt. Miller died today.

Pressing into rotten mud,
turning red with precious blood.
Life flows out and stains the ground
before departing without sound.

And then at last the fury's hushed,
machine guns silenced in the dusk.
Could this then be the longest day?
Lt. Miller died today.

By PFC Arthur D. Gardner

"The Unknown"

I

The stars in the sky to us here below,
are jewels high in heaven
By God's hand they're sown.
To lead us, to guide us, and show us the way,
To righteousness--freedom, --to live as we may.

II

To know what the stars, the sun, or the earth,
What mortal may guess at the mystery of birth?
To live and to breathe, then to die--, is our worth,
Yet crowning it all is death's shadow --, our curse

III

We know not, we care not, we dare not to stress,
What happens to souls that are taken by death.
'Tis better, far better, to live --, and refrain
From perpetually pondering what's to lose -- or to gain.

IV

Are we born of the earth and reared through the years
To die -- and be nothing? How wretched our fears!
God help us! Our weakness! Our puny desires!
To be wracked by our knowledge of eternal hell fires!

By PFC Arthur D. Gardner

"Thoughts"

I

The thoughts we think are always linked
with our sub-conscious mind,
So law and justice must come first,
before your thoughts or mine.
Have you ever thought to rob a bank?
Commit the perfect crime?
To let your thoughts degrade themselves,
along an evil line.

II

Our thoughts are tools that Satan rules,
they're his---
Unless we know our mind
and think of thoughts like these---
A clear cool morning in the spring,
of joy and golden laughter,
A flower nodding at our feet,
a queenly child of Nature.

III

The gentle rains that come again
to fresh the thirsty land,
Of lordly trees and waterfalls,
as well as wastes of sand,
Such thoughts as these can only leave
our minds so pure and wrought,
That evil thoughts must take to wing
and never more be thought.

By PFC Arthur D. Gardner

"TROOP TRANSPORT"

I

There's something about a transport that preys upon your mind,
It soon would drive you batty, if you are so inclined.
It matters very little if you're veteran or recruit,
No difference who the Skipper is, we know he is a brute!

II

They have their rules and regulations, enough to drive men mad,
We cannot smoke in quarters, which also makes us mad.
We can't sit here, we can't sit there, they are always on our necks.
It's "You can't sit there Marine, for you clutter up the deck!

III

The heat is suffocating, the tropic sun boils down.
It's nothing to the Nave, they look on us and frown,
"I told you once Marine, and I'll not tell you again,
The next time you sit in that patch of shade,
I'll kick your bloody shins!!"

IV

What can we do? What can we say? 'Tis all of no avail.
She's a Navy ship and Navy law will see her through to hell!
We can beat our chops and bite our nails, and wish they all were dead
When we snooze into our hammocks, and think of home --- and bed.

V

I've mentioned all these things to you, hoping you would see,
That life aboard a transport is hardly one of glee.
This shaving in saltwater, to me is out of date.
But those infernal "beans for breakfast" are what I really hate!

By PFC Arthur D. Gardner

"THIS IS IT"

I

We stormed upon the beaches, we killed a thousand Japs,
I guess we fired a million rounds, on our trek around the
map.
No matter what the outfit, no matter where they hit,
You're sure to hear these very words, "Well boys, this is it!"

II

To you they may mean nothing, to us they mean a lot.
For we never use those tragic words, except when things get
hot.
We leave the ship at "H" hour, clamber down the net,
Into a waiting Higgins boat, and we know that --- "This is
it!"

III

The Naval guns are booming, they're really on the beam,
They score a hit right on the Nips, we hear the bastards
scream!
We're getting closer – closer now, we're matching unit for
unit,
I look at Joe and try to grin, He whispers --- "This is it!"

IV

We're nearly to the coral beach, the boat grates on the sand,
The ramp is down, we're running out, the Japs are close at
hand!
The mortars now are worst of all, they chew your flesh to
bits,
I'm afraid to run, but I can't stay here, Oh God yes --- "This
is it!"

V

I see my Buddy dying – now he's lying cold and still,
Tho' I am safely on the beach, 'twas him that paid the bill.
We slowly push the Jap horde back, 'Till they're as far as
they can get.
And as they see us coming on, they too know – "This is it."

By PFC Arthur D. Gardner

"HAVE YOU KNOWN"

I

Have you looked Death in the eye?
Have you seen him standing by?
With his horrid grinnin' silence-
In his hands your heart to tear.

II

Have you known the boundless fear
That you wouldn't long be here?
Upon the earth, to taste once more,
Of life that's held so dear.

III

Have you felt the burning wrath
From the torrid lungs of Death?
As it fanned your cheek,
Or rent the air near-by?

IV

I've discovered this, --- Aye, this;
From deaths impartial kiss; -
You can't know what it is to live,
'Till you've known what it is to die!

By PFC Arthur D. Gardner

"THROUGH THE BOLTED DOOR"

Perhaps you've heard the morbid tale,
That came to me midst the stench of ale,
From The painted lips of an erstwhile beaut
In a gambling house of ill repute.

I'd sat at the bar but a scant half hour
When I chanced to see this faded flower--
Where she sat alone with eyes downcast,
As a bruised beaten Sailor before the mast.

The very depths of despair were there,
In the hallow eyes and stringy hair,
To the sagging mouth that once had smiled
Or laughed aloud as a carefree child.

There in that smoky, half dim light,
My eyes were shocked by the touching sight
Of a girl gone wrong and sank so low
As to sell her body, thus selling her soul!

I tore my eyes away from her
To glance askance at the bolted door,
For I meant to leave, 'ere my wounded thoughts
Should prompt me to speak with this girl of naught.

But as I left my seat to walk away,
I thought to look once more her way,
For her face was there upon my mind, –
Not cold, and hard, --- but soft, and kind.

An innocent face with great brown eyes,
And firm red lips that never lied,
With sweet dark hair, that laid in folds,
By the Roguish wind, that lover bold.

A clear frank face with naught to hide,
As the innocent gaze of a new-wed bride.
A budding rose that blooms at last,
Or a Holy Nun so pure and chaste.

I stumbled then and the thoughts were gone.
As the last dim star at the break of dawn.
And I looked again at the woman there
With the hollow eyes and stringy hair.

Now she raised her eyes from the glass of beer,
And her eyes met mine in cold numb fear.
As my steps were turned by an unseen hand
Toward this wretch forever damned.

Damned forever by good or bad,
Wisely ignored by hero and cad,
For who should be seen in public sight,
With a devil's wench who knows no right?

In a darkened room with shuttered pane,
A man could laugh and boast, -- in vain.
For such a woman knows, as well as sin,
When once in the light he'll be silent again.

That is the fate she must accept,
To bow the head that once has slept,
Upon another's loving breast,
Long 'ere the babe itself has guessed.

The fate that is what she's to be,
Long after she leaves her mother's knee.
To be steeped in sin, betrayed and mocked,
Then cast aside, when she loved --- and lost!

She half arose as I came near,
Disgust replaced her look of fear, --
"Go away you fool, and let me stay
Here like a lady while once I may!"

She sank back down upon the chair
And fixed me with an anguished stare,
As I heeded not her whispered plea,
But placed myself where I oughtn't to be.

"May the Devil have mercy on you Sir,
May God prevent that 'ere you were,
Admitted through the gates of light
We make you pay for your sins this night".

For I've told you plain that I want you not,
With no price on earth may my body be bought.
"What's that you say? I know you lie!
You want my body, what else would you buy?"

"You make me laugh, I've heard your line.
I've heard them all in my short time.
But if sit you must, then keep you still,
I'll show you a coward I'm going to kill!"

"I see there pity in your eyes,
I don't want your pity, I don't want your lies.
Don't tell me I should be mother and wife,
My soul may be gone but I've still got my life!"

"How did I come to be as you see me here,
An ugly old hag all sotted with beer?
You needn't protest, I know what you mean,
Let's speak with the facts, my soul's past redeem

"

Once I had a mother sir, lovely as yours,
And a good honest father, though modestly poor,
I was raised with religion and a firm gentle hand,
How should they know I'd be ruined by a man?

I knew not of lies, I'd heard not a one.
Until he came along with a million and one.
And I a mere child, a fool I was,
To listen to his lies as a woman does.

I'll spare you the details, you've heard them all,
The steps we take before we fall,
He wronged me, broke me, and then was gone,
When I needed him most, when the baby was born.

I was turned from the door, they'd not let me in,
My family disowned me for one thoughtless sin.
What's that you ask? My baby you say?
I've seen it no more, it was taken away.

And now Sir, I beg you, to go your way,
In a few short moments, a debt will be paid,
For from that time until this night,
I've not lain eyes on a more welcome sight.

Then an hour ago, as I opened that door,
For there stood the man I've thought about more
Through the years of my weakness and sin,
Then I've thought put together the rest of the men!

Then he left me alone, I was broken and hurt,
The hurt is still there, I'd be dead if it weren't.
For its kept me alive to repay the debt,
That cost me so much. 'Twas my honor he bet!

95

Behind you Sir, with his woman and gin,
Is the man I spoke of; may God pity him!
He remembers me not, for I've changed a lot,
Since the day when he left me to die and to rot

But I fooled him Sir, I still live on,
While he's as helpless as a new born fawn!
So saying, she rose, as sure as Death,
While I sat frozen with bated breath.

While a pistol was drawn from beneath her sleeve
And aimed at the man who had caused her grief.
The shot rang clear as the tone of a bell,
And I knew 'ere I looked, the man had fell!

The man? Yes, he's dead, and buried as well,
Perhaps he's repenting now, somewhere in Hell.
Of the girl - - I've heard nothing, she was seen never more,
Since she passed, unmolested, through the bolted door!

By PFC Arthur D. Gardner

"TO LOVE TOO WELL"

A lovely Maid of long ago
With face so fair and hair of gold,
Reposed with languor, in the shade
A great oak tree, of splendor made
She dreamed of lovers, far and near,
Of Knights who'd risk their lives for her,
Indeed a few lay cold and dead,
Where love of her their steps had led
Then into battle where they fall!
Alas! In vain, loved too well!

II

She spurned their love and bid them go,
To find a maid whose thoughts were slow
Enough to Wed one such as they,
And spend their life along life's way.
'Twas not for she, for she was Fair,
With no desire to age with care!
She smiled at them with eyes like wine,
While her lips etched words on drunken Minds!
They rode away with heads bowed low,
And the Maiden laughed to see them go!

III

Thus things went on and as that time drew near,
When the maid must find her Lord or peer,
For the years slipped by and day by day,
The maid new well her charms would fade!
One day In Spring she met the one,
She'd been seeking for, since time began.
She wooed him with her sweetest smiles,
He scoffed her love, and kissed to tell!
Alas! In vain, she loved too well!

By PFC Arthur D. Gardner

"WE ARE THE LAST OF THE RAIDERS"

Throw away your boots and knives,
They're going to end our Raider lives,
They're doing away with the best they've got,
And throwing us in with the common lot.

Away with all your sentiments,
They're going to try to make us, gents,
By sticking us into Regiments,
For we are the last of the Raiders.

We eat bum chow, we have no socks,
Just ammunition in our packs,
We've never seen the Waves or WAAC's,
For we are the last of the Raiders.

Twenty-one months and still no leave,
On Bougainville on Christmas Eve,
When we leave, the Corps will grieve,
For we are the last of the Raiders.

The 4th Marines have got our lot,
And every day there is more hot cock,
And still we sit on this damn rock,
For we are the last of the Raiders.

First, we're Jekyll, and then we're Hyde,
We'll never see that old Stateside,
Our whole Battalion, got shanghaied,
For we are the last of the Raiders.

So, throw away your Raider schemes,
And throw away your Raider dreams,
We're going to join the 4th Marines,
For we are the last of the Raiders.

There's only one thing that makes us gloat,
Because of all the things that float,
We hate a God damn rubber boat,
For we are the last of the Raiders.

So, throw away your B.A.R.'s,
And love the BAM's and SPAR's,
And spend your time in Stateside bars,
For you are no more a Raider.

By PFC Arthur D. Gardner

PFC Arthur Don Gardner

Drawing by PFC Arthur Don Gardner

Drawings by PFC Arthur Don Gardner

Drawing by PFC Arthur Don Gardner

SECOND LIEUTENANT JACK MILLER AUG 1942, 2A, (WIA 03
DEC, DOW 04 DEC 1942). Photo taken in Happier Days be-
fore MAKIN ISLAND RAID while at Camp Catlin, Hawaii.
Photo Courtesy COL CLELAND EARLY

Printed in the USA
CPSIA information can be obtained
at www.ICGtesting.com
LVHW090547171123
763818LV00070B/1241/J

9 781716 218248